THE PROBLEM WITH NURSE EMMA

BY

SOFONDA WOOD

Chapter 1

Emma planted her skis in the snow and looked about her. Something seemed odd. There was a strong sense of déjà vu. Had she been here before? No, it wasn't déjà vu; that's the feeling that one has lived through a situation before. What she felt was something more than déjà vu; it wasn't just a feeling; it was a knowing. She knew she had been there before, in that place and at that very moment. There was the sense of impending doom; a growing fear in the pit of her stomach. Something awful was about to happen, but what it was eluded her.

She looked up the ski slope in anticipation. At any moment Brock would come bounding over the hill. Something inside her dreaded seeing him and she prayed that he would not come; but a second later there he was. He came springing over the hill, taking to the air momentarily as he did.

When he raced past her Brock leaned onto the edge of his skis, spraying the cold snow powder in her face as he went. Glancing back, he laughed loudly when he saw her dusting the snow off her face.

"Race you down!" He called back to her then leaned forward into the skis to pick up speed.

With a push from the poles she darted after him. She was an experienced skier but not as fast as Brock, and much more cautious. By the time she could get moving he was already over the next knoll and out of her vision. He was going too fast, she thought. From previous runs she remembered that just ahead there was a clump of trees and the ski slope took a turn. Brock was going way too fast to safely make the bend.

When she got to the top of the next hill, she saw the group of trees, but she didn't see Brock. He couldn't have gotten that far ahead, she thought. Stopping halfway down the hill, she paused and looked around but didn't see him anywhere. She spotted the fresh ski tracks in the new fallen snow and began to slowly follow them toward the patch of trees. All the while a sense of dread grew in her gut. For a moment she thought he was hiding behind a tree, waiting to jump out and frighten her, but deep inside she knew better.

She glided through the trees following the ski tracks until they ended right at a fallen tree. She unclipped her skis from her boots so she could climb over it. Then she saw Brock lying in the snow just behind the heavy trunk. He was on his side and motionless; one of his legs was twisted into an awkward position and a sharp bone was piercing through his pant leg just above the knee. Blood stained the snow extending nearly a foot beyond where he lay. When the bone broke and pierced the skin, it had torn open an artery causing blood to spurt from the wound.

"Brock!" She cried out and fell to the ground next to him. She pulled his head and shoulders onto her lap.

As he gasped for breath, he looked up at her, but his eyes didn't seem to focus. He tried to speak, but no words came from his mouth. There was a deep laceration on the side of his head and blood streamed from his ear.

"Brock! You're okay! You'll be okay!" She began to rock him back and forth. "Please, baby. You'll be okay."

Desperately she twisted around in all directions looking for someone, but they were alone. She screamed. "Help! Someone please help us!

Brock's breathing became shallow and rapid. His back arched slightly as if he were in pain. She knew he was near death. She had to do something to help him, but she had no idea what to do.

"Help!" She screamed again.

Brock's eyes drifted up and fixed toward the sky. He breathed in a deep sigh then exhaled heavily and he fell motionless and limp. Emma watched his chest in horror, waiting for another breath that would never come. His eyes became fixed and dilated, and she watched helpless as he slipped away. Brock died there as Emma rocked him in her arms.

"No! No! No!" She cried out.

In the darkness of her bedroom, Emma jolted upright in her bed. The dream had seemed so real it left her disoriented and confused. She shook her head and clinched her fists in an effort to push the dream from her mind.

"Are you ok?" Jennifer, her roommate, flipped on the light and stood in the doorway.

Emma could not respond. She buried her head in her hands and began to cry. No matter how many times she had that dream, it still horrified her. Each time was vivid and in full color, as if she was there, reliving the event over and over again. She saw the bright red blood splatter over the pure white snow; she felt the cold, and she watched the light fade from Brock's eyes. For Emma, it was as painful as if she had experience Brock's death for the first time.

Jennifer climbed on the bed and hugged her. "It's all right. It was only a dream." She held Emma in her arms and rocked her back and forth until the tears had subsided.

"I'm all right," Emma said through her sobbing. "I'm sorry to wake you."

"You want to talk about it?"

"It was just —" Emma stammered. "I dreamed about Brock again. When it happened."

"Oh baby. I'm so sorry." Jennifer hugged her again. "I was afraid working at the hospital might stir up those memories. Are you sure you're up for it?"

"Yes. I have to do this, for him." Emma looked at the clock. It was 3:00 a.m. She still had a couple hours before she needed to get ready for work.

"You want me to stay with you?"

"If you don't mind."

Jennifer clicked off the light and the two girls snuggled under the blanket. Within a few minutes, Jennifer was sound asleep while Emma stared into the darkness. She remembered the dream vividly and tried to recall the way Brock looked as he laughed and skied past her; the way he looked before the accident. She hugged her pillow and remembered him as he was in life. Despite the sorrow she felt from the dream, the memory of Brock's touch stayed with her and it was that memory she clung to as she drifted back to sleep.

The next morning the tires on her old VW Beetle screeched as it rounded the corner into the hospital parking lot. The vehicle had barely come to a stop when the driver's side door burst open and Emma jumped out. She glanced at her watch, then bounded toward the employee entrance.

Inside the building, Emma raced down the hallway to the time clock, grabbed a time card and punched in for her first day of work as a Registered Nurse. Across from the employee's time clock was a full-length mirror. She took a moment to inspect herself, appreciating the crisp white nursing uniform that consisted of a white dress, a pinafore apron and a nursing cap. It was a very traditional nursing uniform, to some it would appear old-fashioned, but Emma loved the way she looked wearing it. Satisfied she was presentable, she proceeded down the hallway toward the Head Nurse's office. She paused before going outside taking one last opportunity to smooth out her skirt, a nervous habit she had developed as a student.

A plump little nun with rosy cheeks sat behind the reception desk. She wore the traditional nun's black habit; a black full-length tunic, a white wimple that covered her neck and right behind her cheeks, and the black fabric that covered the top of her head.

She peered at Emma over her eye glasses for a moment then a smile swept over her face. "Ah, I remember you, young lady. I'm Sister Faith. Welcome to St. Rita's Hospital. I'm so happy that you have joined our family."

Sister Faith rose and made her way around the desk and greeted her with a warm embrace that caught Emma off guard.

Emma was a little uncomfortable at having her personal space breeched unexpectedly, but the warm show of affection, nevertheless, put her at ease. The nun stepped back and studied the young girl. "You're a pretty little thing. I love your nursing uniform. It's classic. You don't see many young women now days that respect tradition."

"Thank you, ma'am." Having never met a nun she wasn't sure how she should address the Sister, so she made a feeble attempt at a curtsey.

The nun chuckled in amusement at the gesture. "My dear child. I'm a nun, not the queen."

"I'm sorry."

"Give me a moment to check my notes." She returned to her desk and retrieved a clipboard containing a stack of hand-written notes. She adjusted her glasses and flipped through the pages. "You are —" she continued to scan the papers.

"Emma Paige."

"Ah yes, here you are. You're a Registered Nurse?"

"Yes ma'am. This is my first day."

"Oh, please dear, call me Sister Faith."

"Yes, ma'am. I mean yes, Sister… Sister Faith."

The nun continued to study the clipboard. "This says you will be a float nurse?" She pulled her glasses off and looked Emma up and down, sizing her up for the job.

"Yes, Sister Faith. I was told I'd be floating between the Emergency Room and the Intensive Care Unit."

"Very impressive. It takes a special type of person to work in such a stressful environment." Sister Faith looked up and studied Emma again. "If you don't mind my saying, you seem to be a little timid. And you're just a whisper of a girl. How tall are you?"

"I'm 5'4", and much stronger than I look."

"You're a petite little thing, aren't you?" Sister Faith gave her a concerned look, more motherly than judgmental. "Are you sure you know what you're getting yourself into?"

Emma straightened her back and held her head high. "I'm not as timid as I might look. My last clinical rotation was at the county hospital and I did a lot of work in their Emergency Department. I can handle myself once I learn my way around."

"Perhaps you can, dear girl." Sister Faith smiled with satisfaction, happy that despite Emma's youth and petite stature the girl was not a shrinking violet. "Anyhoo, if you'll have a seat, I'll let Mrs. Rose know you've arrived."

Emma nodded politely then sat down in a nearby chair. Mrs. Rose was the person who interviewed her and offered her the job.

Sister Faith picked up the phone and pressed zero. "Good morning, Miss Walters. Can you please page Mrs. Rose to this number? Thank you!"

Almost immediately a voice announced over the hospital PA system. "Mrs. Sandra Rose, please call extension 221. Mrs. Sandra Rose, extension 221."

A moment later the phone rang.

"It's a blessed day in the Nursing Admin office, how may I be of assistance?" Sister Faith said when she answered the call. The nun paused a moment to listen to the caller, then she continued. "Yes, Miss Emma Paige has arrived." Again, she listened, nodding her head all the while. "Oh, is that today? It must have slipped my mind. I can drop Miss Paige off in the ER and then I'll be there directly. Thank you."

Sister Faith hung up the phone then turned to Emma. "Mrs. Rose sends her apologies for not being here to welcome you herself, but she's tied up in meetings this morning. I'm told I should drop you off in the Emergency Room to begin orientation."

"Oh, that'll be great." Emma was eager to start her day. She was nervous but thrilled at the prospect of working in the Emergency Room.

The emergency department was on the same floor as the administration offices, so it took only a moment for them to arrive at the nursing station. The ER was bustling with activity; nurses and staff rushed from room to room like bees in a hive.

"Oh nurse!" Sister Faith stopped the first person she came to wearing scrubs.

"Yes, Sister?" A middle-aged black woman with a slight Jamaican accent was hurrying by, her arms full of medical supplies.

"What's happening?"

"There's been a multi-vehicle accident and several trauma victims are in route."

"Oh dear!"

"I'm sorry, but we're in a rush. Was there something you needed?" The nurse asked.

"Yes. This is Miss Emma —" she struggled to recall her name.

"Paige. Emma Paige."

"Ah, yes. Miss Emma Paige. She's starting today. Mrs. Rose said to bring her to the charge nurse to begin her ER orientation."

"Kenise!" Another nurse stepped out of a nearby trauma room and called to her. "We need an Ambu bag in here!"

"On my way!" Kenise responded, then turned back to Emma. "A pleasure to have you on board."

"Well, I'll leave you in capable hands, Miss Paige," Sister Faith gave a smile then patted Emma on the arm. "Now I must be off."

Before Kenise could lodge a protest, the nun scurried down the hallway and disappeared out the double doors.

"I'm sorry for the inconvenience." Emma could tell Kenise was less than enthusiastic about having an orientee tag along.

"Don't worry 'bout that," Kenise smiled and without warning unloaded the armful of bandages and IV bags to Emma. "Never a perfect time. Here in the ER it's sink or swim when it comes to new staff. We just throw you in and hope you don't go under."

Emma's eyes widened, and she laughed nervously.

"It's all right. Just hang back and observe. We won't let you get in over your head."

Kenise hurried down the hall with Emma following close behind. Inside the trauma room, Kenise motioned toward an empty stretcher in the center of the room. On it was a crisp white sheet and in the center of the bed was a set of electrodes with gray wires leading up to a heart monitor on the wall.

"Just drop the supplies on the bed. I'll stock them in the bins." Kenise laid two bags of saline in front of Emma along with packets of IV tubing. "I'll put up the stock, you can hang the IVs. Make sure to keep the lines sterile."

"Yes, ma'am."

Emma tore the covers from the two bags of saline then retrieved the IV tubing and did the same. She pulled the cover from off the end of the tubing and inserted it into the saline bag before attaching it to the hook on the top of the pole. Then she did the same to the second saline bag.

Kenise was busy inspecting the inventory of a drug cart next to the bed, all the while watching Emma.

"Oh baby, you need to clamp off your lines." Kenise said. "You left your lines wide open."

"Huh?" Emma looked at the IV setups and saw saline spraying from the end of the tubing all over the floor below.

Kenise rushed over and grabbed the IV tubing then clamped the clasp on each of the IV lines until the fluids stopped.

"Oh, I'm sorry. I didn't think about closing the lines." Emma turned red with embarrassment.

"Just a mistake. Grab a towel and dry the floor, will ya? We don't want anybody slipping and falling."

"Of course," Emma retrieved a towel from a linen cart in the corner of the room and squatted down to mop up the floor. "I'm so sorry. I'm really nervous. This is my first real work day and I'm all thumbs."

"It's all right." Kenise smiled as she finished stocking the supply bins. "Where did you work before?"

"I did my clinicals at Scott County General."

"Clinicals!" You mean you're a new grad?" Kenise stopped what she was doing and turned to Emma with her eyebrows raised.

"Yes. This is my first job as a nurse."

"And they hired you for the Emergency Room?" Kenise couldn't hide her shock. Being a high stress work environment, she didn't think the emergency department was any place for a new graduate. She mumbled something under her breath about administration being out in left field.

Emma felt defensive. "Actually, I'll be floating between the intensive care unit and the emergency department."

"Oh girl, no. No, don't let them do that to you," Kenise warned. "You're gonna burn out in a matter of weeks trying to learn all the rules and policies for each of the units. And then there's the stress of every patient you have trying to die on you. Being a trauma nurse or ICU nurse is hard enough, but trying to do both at the same time is insane. And have mercy, you're a new grad to boot. You're not gonna manage it all, especially being fresh out of school."

"I was at the top of my class," Emma protested, "and I'm a quick learner. She was confident in her skills as a nurse and with good reason. She had graduated with honors and had received high praises from all her clinical instructors.

"Honey, I'm not questioning your skills, just your wisdom," Kenise put her hands on her hips and laughed. Next time you apply for a job, you might want to ask why there's an opening in the first place."

"They said it was the only opening available."

"Ha! The only opening!" Kenise's shoulders jiggled up and down as she chuckled with amusement. She shook her head. "Baby, they saw you coming. The last nurse that worked that float position ended up in lock down on the 6th floor."

"6th floor?"

"Yes ma'am. 6th floor. That's the psych ward."

"Don't let her get you all shook up," a heavy-set blonde nurse entered in time to hear part of their conversation. "Miss Jenna ended up on the 6th floor because they promoted her to charge nurse up there."

"Uh huh, so they say." Kenise smirked. "Still, birds of a feather, you know. Poor Jenna bout lost her mind floating between the units and the emergency room."

"I'm Deborah, the charge nurse today. You're our new orientee?"

"Yes, ma'am."

"Don't ma'am me. I clock-in just like you do."

"It's nice to meet you. I'm Emma."

"Sister Faith breezed through and dropped her off," Kenise said.

"Well that'll be fine. Go ahead and shadow Kenise this morning, but don't pay attention to anything she says. Watch what she does and then do the opposite." Deborah chuckled.

"Now Miss Deborah, why you have to say such things?" Kenise laughed. "I'm the best nurse you got. You're lucky I stick around."

"You know I'm messing with you." Deborah gave Kenise a pat on the back then headed for the door. She paused before leaving and looked back to Emma. "I'll get back with you later in the day after things settle down a bit."

"She's a good one, that Miss Deborah," Kenise said after she had left the room. "I've always liked her, but even more now that she's transitioned to a real woman."

Emma's eyes widened in disbelief. "Oh my God. You mean she's transgendered? I would have never thought."

A smile swept over Kenise's face and she began to laugh. "Girl, you know what your problem is? You're green, like you just fell off the back of the turnip truck. You better tighten yourself up round here or they gonna have a field day messin with you."

"What? I don't understand." Emma was confused. She had no idea what a turnip truck was.

"Of course you don't, baby. I'm only teasing, that ain't no man."

"Oh," she said and blushed with embarrassment for being so naïve.

A man in blue scrubs entered the trauma room and flashed a quick smile at the two nurses. Both women focused their attention on the striking figure. He was tall and athletically slender with shoulder-length blonde hair. Emma could not help but stare as he opened the top drawer of the code cart and leaned over searching through the contents. He was beautiful, like watching live art. When he found what he was looking for he stood upright and for a moment he and Emma locked eyes. He swept his hair behind both ears to reveal his piercing green eyes, then he smiled at her before hurrying away.

Emma audibly sighed as she watched him leave, not turning away until he disappeared around a corner.

"Exactly." Kenise sighed as well. "Lord have mercy, if I were 20 years younger or even ten."

"Who is that?"

"He's yummy. He's one of the docs here." When Kenise said he was yummy, she was only referring to him being so handsome. She knew very well that was Dr. Russo, so she was stunned at Emma's response.

"Yummy? That can't be his real name." Emma giggled. "But it does fit him."

Kenise turned away and pretended to be inspecting the monitor, but in reality, she was fighting back the laughter. She couldn't believe that Emma actually thought Dr. Russo's name was Dr. Yummy. On the spur of the moment she decided to take advantage of the situation and have some fun at Emma's expense.

"Yeah, it's Dr. Yummy. I think it's Scandinavian or Russian." Kenise struggled to contain her amusement. She couldn't believe that the poor thing would really believe Dr. Yummy was his real name. Surely Emma wasn't that naïve.

"And he's single too." Kenise watched as Emma became perky at the information. "You have a beau? I don't see any rings."

"No. I'm single."

"A pretty young thing like you? You should have dozens of young men beating on your door."

"Not really. I've been too busy studying to date."

Emma wasn't completely lying, but she wasn't telling the whole truth either. Although she was single, it had little to do with school work; the real reason was that was still heartbroken over Brock. He was her high school sweetheart, and they dated into college. She considered him the love of her life. They were engaged and planned to marry right after graduation. During Brock's final year in college they had taken a ski vacation to Aspen for winter break. It was on that trip that Brock was killed in the skiing accident. She wasn't willing to talk about Brock especially with the dream she had still fresh in her mind. It was too painful to discuss with someone she had just met, so she simply said she wasn't seeing anyone rather than go into the heartbreaking story of her love life.

"Good for you." Kenise was genuinely glad to hear that Emma was serious enough about having a nursing career to forego dating until she was working. "I suppose now that you're a real nurse you'll be wanting to find you a doctor of your own."

"Certainly not!" Emma crossed her arms and scowled at the suggestion. "I didn't spend four years in nursing school to find a man. I plan on doing something with my life."

"Again, I say good for you. There's already too many young girls going into nursing hoping to marry a doctor. Well, enough chit-chat. Help me check this code cart while we have a moment."

The two walked over to the large metal cart that the doctor had examined. Kenise took a clipboard from off the top of the cart and opened the top drawer.

"We need to do a cart check at the beginning of our shift and again after each patient discharge from the room," Kenise explained. "There's nothing worse than needing something during a trauma and finding it missing from the cart. That's the fastest way to piss off a nurse."

"I understand."

"I'll call out the inventory then you check the count. It'll help you get familiar with where things are."

"Sure," Emma agreed.

"Epinephrine 1 to 10,000," Kenise called off. "There should be four syringes marked as 1 milligram to 10 cc's."

Emma checked the drawer until she found the items. "Yes, there's four."

"Atropine, four syringes of 1 milligram to 10 cc's."

"Yes. Four syringes."

They continued the inventory until every item in the drawer had been checked. Just after they finished there was a loud commotion coming from the hallway. Emma looked up to see three paramedics dressed in blue uniforms hurriedly pushing a patient on a stretcher into the room. Behind them came running additional nurses, along with the handsome physician she knew as Dr. Yummy. To Emma, the room seemed to be a turmoil.

"Honey, why don't you step away so you can observe," Kenise said as she took her by the arm to guide her out of the way. "Just hang back and watch."

Emma stepped to the wall where she could see the trauma team go to work. She realized that what initially appeared to be turmoil was anything but chaos. Each member of the trauma team worked in a well-organized, coordinated effort. Each knowing their specific task and performing their duties in a harmonized effort. Emma marveled at the team work, it was like the internal workings of a clock. Each part, or caregiver, having a specific duty they performed in unison. They performed a well-orchestrated dance; each movement rehearsed and precise.

Using a board, the team transferred the patient from the stretcher to the bed. Then one nurse pulled electrode wires from off the patient's chest, while another replaced them with the electrodes from the overhead monitor. At the same time the doctor listened to the patient's breath sounds as Kenise cut away the patient's clothing with a pair of heavy scissors.

An endotracheal tube protruded from the patient's mouth and was attached to a ventilation bag which one of the paramedics squeezed intermittently. With each squeeze of the bag, the patient's chest rose and fell in a natural rhythm.

"What do we have?" Dr. Russo asked the paramedics.

A paramedic responded. "34-year-old white male on the receiving end of a multi-vehicle accident. No known medical history. Prior to our arrival at the scene, the victim had been extricated from the vehicle by first responders and was laying prone on the road. He was alert but disoriented and complained of severe chest pain and shortness of breath. Physical exam showed massive bruising on the victim's chest. Multiple rib fractures are palpable bilaterally. Vital signs were; heart rate 110, respirations 28, BP 100 over 55, pulses weak but steady at 2+.

"In route the victim became unresponsive and apneic. Tachycardic at 145 with dropping BP. We intubated using an 8.0 endotracheal tube. Breath sounds were bilateral and equal, and a CO2 detector confirmed placement."

Russo examined the patient as the paramedic gave his report. There was extensive bruising on the patient's chest and using only the slightest pressure, he could feel the broken ribs beneath the skin. The heart rate on the monitor showed 142. It was a steady, but rapid rate; what Emma recognized as tachycardia. She noticed frequent irregular beats that had a much wider wave form than the others. These she readily identified as premature ventricular contractions, or PVCs. She recalled from class that these PVCs were not that unusual, especially for a traumatic injury. As she watched the scene play out, she reviewed what she had learned in nursing school.

"No pulse," Dr. Russo announced as he held two fingers against the patient's neck. He placed his stethoscope in his ears and placed the bell of the instrument over the patient's heart. "Hold ventilations," he ordered.

The respiratory therapist at the head of the bed stopped squeezing the Ambu bag.

The doctor closed his eyes and listened, moving the bell of the stethoscope from one spot to another.

"Continue ventilations," he said, and the therapist resumed his cadenced squeezing of the Ambu bag.

"Someone start compressions, we have PEA folks," Dr. Russo said in a loud voice to make certain everyone on the team would hear him.

One paramedic used his foot to position a small step stool at the side of the bed then stepped upon it. He placed his hand carefully in the middle of the victim's chest right below the nipple line, then he began compressing the victim's chest at a rapid pace.

PEA, Emma recalled, was the acronym for persistent electrical activity; the condition when there's a heart rate but no detectable pulse. She smiled to herself for knowing the answer, but then felt horrible for smiling while someone was struggling for life just a few feet away.

"And what can cause PEA?" The doctor quizzed the team.

"Trauma. Tension pneumothorax." A nurse answered.

"Cardiac tamponade." Another added.

There was a moment of silence as the staff mentally struggled to remember the remaining causes.

"You guys don't remember your H and T's?" Dr. Russo accused. "Do we need an ACLS refresher course?"

He again placed his stethoscope on the patient's chest and listened first on one side then the other. "Breath sounds are diminished over the right lung field."

He hung the stethoscope back around his neck then proceeded to palpitate the victim's neck. "There's a slight tracheal deviation toward the left. What does that make us suspect? Decreased breath sounds on the right with trachea deviation toward the opposing lung?"

"Right tension pneumothorax," the entire team answered in unison.

"Right," Dr. Russo responded. "Let's get a chest tube ready."

Kenise and another nurse began ripping open bags and setting up for the procedure.

"Any other ideas?" The doctor asked the team.

"Hypovolemia," Emma spoke up. All eyes turned to see her for the first time standing against the wall. She was self-conscious as if she had just made a big mistake in front of the team. Everyone looked at her expectantly.

"I mean, well, he's had a traumatic injury. A tension pneumothorax can cause PEA on its own, but there's also the likelihood of internal bleeding."

"Good answer! Two points to the student nurse." Dr. Russo nodded his approval. "Hang 2 liters of lactated Ringer's solution and run it wide open."

"The x-ray tech is here," Kenise announced as a female technician pushed the large portable x-ray machine into the room.

Suddenly, the heart monitor began to alarm. On the monitor screen where there had been a regular EKG rhythm, there was now a rapid saw-tooth pattern.

"We have V-tack!" Kenise shouted and immediately pulled the code cart to the bedside and grabbed the defibrillator.

She passed the paddles to Dr. Russo then she then tore open a packaged containing two large gel pads. She slapped one pad on the right side of the chest just above the nipple line and the other on the patient's left side at the lower section of the rib cage. Once the pads were in place, Russo pressed both defibrillator paddles firmly against each pad on the patient.

"Charge to 200 joules," Russo said.

Kenise pushed the red button on the face of the defibrillator and there was a high-pitched tone that grew in increasing intensity as the electrical charge raised to the set level.

"Clear!" The doctor called out loudly. Everyone stepped away from the stretcher and raised their hands in the air. He surveyed the team and once he was satisfied that no one was in contact with the patient or stretcher, he discharged the defibrillator.

There was an audible thump as the defibrillator discharged and the patient's entire body spasmed from the shock. In unison everyone turned to gaze at the heart monitor. For a moment there was a flat line across the screen and then the heart rate reappeared. The monitor showed a normal beat tracing but with a rapid rate of 150 beats per minute.

The doctor handed the paddles back to Kenise then checked for a pulse, first in the carotid area of the neck and then in the patient's groin area over the femoral artery.

"No pulse," he pronounced after a moment. "Start compressions. Ok people, let's do this straight by the ACLS algorithm. Give 1 milligram of epi then repeat in 5 minutes."

Kenise motioned for Emma to come to help. Hesitantly, she made her way to the bedside. She was timid, nervous to be put on the spot in front of the entire trauma team.

"Get the epi from the top drawer," Kenise instructed. "I need you to give it rapid IV push through the IV port," Kenise instructed. Can you do that?"

"Yes." Her voice cracked a little and her mouth became dry.

Emma took the box containing the epinephrine from the cart and ripped it open. Though she had given medications many times during her clinical training, her hands were trembling. This was not practice on a manikin, it was a real patient in critical condition.

She took a deep cleansing breath then wiped the IV port with an alcohol pad then inserted the syringe into the port. Emma looked at Kenise for approval that she was doing it correctly and after receiving an approving nod, she injected the syringe into the IV line.

"You need to flush with saline." Kenise reminded her.

"Oh, yeah." Emma took a syringe of saline and injected it into the same port so the epinephrine would flush completely through the tubing and into the patient's vein.

"Very good," Kenise said. "And always call out the medication and dosage so the recorder can enter it on the code sheet."

"Oh, I'm sorry," Emma replied. "One milligram of 1 to 10,000 Epinephrine in."

Deborah, the charge nurse, stood in the doorway with a clipboard. She looked at the clock and called out, "Epi given at 0747," then wrote the time on the code sheet.

Emma was processing the trauma in her mind and asking herself how to help this poor victim. He was dying before her eyes, and she felt helpless. She looked at his face, except for the breathing tube that was sticking out his mouth the poor man looked like he was only sleeping. He was a young man around her own age, maybe a little older. He reminded her of Brock, not so much by his appearance but by the circumstances. Had Brock only had access to emergency medical care maybe he would have lived.

She looked at the patient and her heart ached for him. It ached for those he would leave behind. She wondered if he had a fiancé who would feel the same loss she has suffered. She wanted him to wake up, not to die like this, with tubes sticking out his mouth and wires and IV tubing dangling off him. He should die an old man surrounded by loved ones, not bloody and battered, and laying naked in a group of strangers.

She continued to search her mind, reviewing all she had learned of traumatic chest injuries in nursing school. She saw the dense bruising, the broken ribs, and considered the lack of pulse. What causes PEA? She asked herself and mentally reviewed the list of things that could cause a heart rate with no pulse. She was so deep in thought she didn't hear the doctor speaking to her until he started to yell.

"Damn it nurse!" He shouted at her. "Are you going to give the second dose of epi or stand there like a moron!"

"Oh, sorry doctor." She retrieved the second dose from the cart and injected it into the IV port.

"One milligram of 1 to 10,000 epi by IV push," she called out to the charge nurse who was continuing to keep records.

"If you can't keep up, then step aside. This is not the time or place for hand holding a student nurse," Russo snapped at Kenise.

"I'm sorry. I'm not a student." Emma shot back.

He didn't acknowledge her apology but instead focused back on checking the pulse. "Hold compressions."

He pressed his finger over the carotid again then the femoral artery.

Feeling no pulse, Russo ordered to resume compressions. He continued to feel for a pulse and from his expression he couldn't find one even with chest compressions occurring.

Emma cowered after receiving her scolding, but she was even more determined to prove herself. She pondered the situation and reviewed what she recalled about hypovolemia. If the patient was bleeding internally, that would explain why the pulses were weak even with compressions. There was not enough blood circulating.

"Dr. Yummy! What about blood products?" Emma said. "Maybe you should give him some blood along with the Ringer's Lactate."

The whole room fell silent except for the heart monitor and the sound of the paramedic performing compressions. She felt completely exposed as all eyes were on her and she thought she even heard one nurse gasp. She looked around at the stunned looks from the team. One of the paramedics turned away and made a weak attempt at hiding his amusement. Was her suggestion that far off base to warrant such a response from the entire team, she wondered?

"What did you say?" The doctor demanded.

"Oh lord," Kenise mumbled and hung her head. She neglected to tell Emma she was joking about the doctor's name. She never dreamed the girl would be so simple-minded as to call him that to his face.

The color drained from Emma's face and she stood frozen, unsure of what she had done to elicit gasps and gawking from the doctor and the trauma team. "I — uh — I mean, if he's bleeding internally then wouldn't packed red blood cells be better than Ringer's lactate?"

"No shit!" Russo glared at her. "The patient most likely has a traumatic aortic dissection, so excuse me if I'm not in the mood for schoolgirl nonsense."

"But Dr. Yummy —" she started to protest. For the first time she saw the embroidered name on his scrub top and the realization stuck her like a slap in the face. Her upper lip began to quiver, and tears shimmered in her eyes when she saw the name Dr. Finn Russo embroidered on his scrub top.

Seeing Emma's tears about to flow pushed Dr. Russo to his boiling point. He had no patience for horseplay in his ER, and even less for crying nurses. So, when he saw Emma start to cry, he lost all remaining patience.

"Get out!" He shouted at Emma. "Get the hell out of my trauma room."

Emma jumped as he shouted at her, yet she stood frozen in her spot. She was ashamed and mortified. How could he scream at her like that, and in front of the entire staff? She wanted to say something. Actually, she wanted to slap him.

"I said get out!".

Emma burst into uncontrollable sobbing and ran from the room, down the hallway, then out the emergency room doors.

CHAPTER 2

Sitting on a bench outside the Emergency Room entrance where the ambulances parked, Emma leaned forward with her face in her hands and cried. This job was so important to her; it was her first position out of nursing school, and she was thrilled for the opportunity to work in a fast-paced critical care area. Most of her classmates had difficulty finding what she considered the good jobs. Of course, with the nursing shortage they all had landed jobs quickly, but in what she thought was entry-level positions like a doctor's offices, nursing homes or on general care floors.

It was typical for new grads to take positions in non-critical areas and later ease into the more critical nursing areas. Emma, on the other hand, was eager for the thrill of trauma care. It wasn't only the excitement she craved, but she needed to make a difference and be able to see the results.

She wanted the satisfaction of helping people and seeing the results of her efforts short term. That was where she wanted to be, in the heat of a life and death struggle where she could truly make a difference and see immediate results of her actions.

She had turned down several opportunities waiting for the right one to come along. There were several good offers, each well-paying and some with weekends and holidays off. But she was determined to work in trauma care. She wanted to be an emergency room nurse where she could save lives. If she was completely honest with herself, she'd realize that her driving force was not just to save lives but to atone for her inability to save Brock. In her heart she believed that if she could save one person the pain of losing a loved one, it would somehow free her of her guilt.

Continuing to monitor the online job boards for trauma nursing positions, she applied for every opening she saw. Most hospitals responded to her application, but only with an offer to interview her for a general care position. Most trauma nurse positions required applicants with prior experience. Still she persisted, until finally St. Rita's called her for an interview.

St. Rita's was a Catholic hospital and a Level I trauma center. As a Catholic herself, she knew the story of St. Rita and had a great fondness for her. According to the legend, St Rita had longed to be a nun since early childhood, but her parents forced her into an unhappy marriage where she endured years in an abusive relationship. After the murder of her husband and two sons, Rita petitioned to enter the monastery of Saint Mary Magdalene in Cascia. Although the convent acknowledged Rita's good character and piety, they feared being associated with the scandal of her husband's violent death, so they turned Rita away. As the story goes, during the night an angel miraculously transported Rita and left her inside the courtyard of the convent. Upon finding her there the next morning, the nuns allowed her to remain. Because of her determination and the obstacles she faced on her journey, Saint Rita is recognized as the patron saint of impossible causes.

Because of Emma's struggle to get into the nursing program and the difficulty in finding a job as a trauma nurse, she felt a connection to St. Rita, and she identified with her plight.

She had first considered nursing when she graduated high school, so she applied to several nursing programs only to find herself rejected and placed on extensive waiting lists. It was disappointing but not exactly devastating, since she didn't really know what she wanted to do as a career. So instead of college, Emma opted to take a job at a fast-food restaurant to save money until she could decide what degree she wanted to pursue.

While she continued to save money, Brock attended college on a football scholarship. They continued to date and became more and more serious. By Brock's sophomore year Emma was still undecided about her future except when it came to her relationship with Brock. When Brock finally proposed, she gave up all thoughts of attending college and instead focused on planning their wedding. They were to marry in two years when he had graduated, so she had a limited amount of time to plan the wedding. College would just simply have to wait.

The winter of Brock's senior year, and only six months before their wedding, Emma and Brock went away with friends for a long ski weekend. That was the weekend that tragedy struck, and it forever changed Emma's life.

After the devastating accident, Emma spent months in mourning. Unable to work, unable to be with friends, unable to forgive herself. She blamed herself for Brock's death. Not because she believed the accident was her fault, but because she could not save him. He died in her arms as she sat helpless, not knowing what to do to help him. As the months passed, Emma became determined that she would never be helpless again. She decided to pursue nursing, and in doing so, redeem herself. If she could save one life and help prevent one person from suffering the loss she had lived, then maybe she could finally heal herself.

Emma reapplied to nursing school. Not just to one program, but to every program within the state. All her applications were rejected except for one that placed her on their waiting list. She was disappointed but still she did not give up. Emma knew in her heart that eventually she would be accepted into a program, whether it took a year or another ten. She worked as a waitress, saving everything she could for the day she would need it for tuition.

The following year she again applied for every nursing program within a 50-mile radius. Every day she ran to the mailbox and hoped; but one letter after another brought disappointment. More rejection letters, and more waiting lists.

Although she was not a straight-A student, she had a strong grade point average with all the program prerequisites. She didn't understand why she was continually getting rejected. So, she decided it was time to ask.

On her day off, she drove to the closest university where she had applied and asked to see the director of the nursing program. Luckily, she got the meeting. Emma introduced herself and pointedly asked why she had been rejected for the nursing program. The director gave her the canned answer she had heard so many times in the rejection letters; more qualified applicants with a limited number of seats available. But as luck would have it, the director had just received word that one of the nursing students had failed to enroll which left an opening in the program. Seeing Emma's determination, the director offered her the opening and Emma accepted on the spot.

After leaving the director's office Emma went straight to admissions and enrolled in the nursing program. She even wrote a check for her first semester's tuition. And, as they say, the rest is history.

Four years later, Emma graduated the top of her class and passed the nursing boards with nearly a perfect score. When it came to her job search, she was as persistent and determined to find the perfect job as she was at getting into the nursing program. She refused to settle for any position other than as a critical care nurse.

Now, she sat on a bench just outside the hospital; completely devastated for fear she was about to be fired after less than two hours on her first day of work.

"Hey, you okay?" A male voice disturbed her.

She was startled to see a paramedic standing a few feet away. He was one of the team that had brought in the trauma patient, and who, unfortunately, had also witnessed her humiliation and eviction from the trauma room.

She looked away in shame. "What do you think?"

"Well, your eyes are swollen and bloodshot. Your hair is matted to your face from tears, and you're sitting here like you're waiting to be executed. I'd say you're not doing so well."

"Wow," she replied. "You must be a psychic or something."

He sat on the opposite end of the bench. She shifted her position away from him to avoid making eye contact. They both sat in silence.

"I'm David. David Marshall." He said after a moment.

Emma halfway glanced over at him but didn't respond. Ashamed and angry, she was too busy wallowing in her own self-pity to make conversation. She sniffed and pulled the long strands of hair that had escaped her ponytail back away from her face.

"Don't take it so bad. You might not believe this, but Dr. Russo has thrown me out of his trauma room twice in the last year." David leaned back casually and placed his arms over his head like he was bragging.

Emma looked directly at him for the first time. He flashed her a grin, then his entire face committed to a big smile. He wasn't a pretty boy; he was ruggedly handsome man. He had that military style masculinity with a buzzed haircut, broad shoulders, and strong arms; the type of man one would expect to see playing the lead in a Hollywood war movie. But there was a tender side to him as well, with dark piercing eyes that sparkled when he smiled at her.

She smiled back at him. Though she felt miserable, something about David put her at ease and she found herself warming up to him.

"Yep," he continued and stretched his long legs out and leaned further back on the bench. "According to Dr. Russo, I'm unprofessional and disrespectful."

She giggled then quickly covered her mouth.

"That's right. You're looking at a real bad boy here."

She smiled. "And what did you do to incur his wrath?"

David sat upright and turned so he was facing her. "Well, the first time happened when I brought in an MVA and during report I referred to the patient as being FOS complicated by 'status dramaticus'."

"I'm sorry, I don't understand those terms."

"New, huh? Is this your first job or first time in the ER?"

"Both," Emma admitted. "I guess it's obvious. I graduated a couple months ago."

"I thought so, you have that deer in the headlights look," he chuckled. "Well, the patient had been in a minor MVA… which means a motor vehicle accident. His car was barely dented, but he was in the middle of the road, writhing in agony, grabbing his neck and back, complaining of chest pain… you know, every injury he could think to fake. The guy groaned and moaned the entire drive to the ER. When we got to the hospital, and he saw the staff, he started even louder with his wailing. Well, Doc Russo shows up and I'm giving the report and I say the patient was a FOS post motor vehicle accident victim complicated by status dramaticus. FOS being the acronym for 'full of shit' and status dramaticus meaning creating drama and exaggerating his injuries."

Emma laughed aloud. "That's terrible."

"Russo thought it was terrible too. He screamed at me for being unprofessional and threw me out."

"How awful!" Emma continued to laugh. For a moment she had forgotten all about being ejected from the trauma room. "But you have to admit that was wrong of you."

"That's nothing. You should hear some of the things nurses have said over patient's beds in the ER. You're in for a rude awakening, missy."

"I imagine that when you deal with life and death situations, making jokes relieves the stress."

"You got that right. If you let yourself wallow in the misery we see every day, you're gonna burn out. Either you find a way to shrug it off, or you'll go home every night crying and end up a drunk."

"No doubt," she agreed.

"So now that the tears are dry, and you seem to have regained yourself, I have to ask; what was that about in there? I mean, the Dr. Yummy thing. You really that smitten with him?"

"No no no, not at all. Kenise told me that was his name." She scoffed and slapped her thigh in frustration. "I can't believe I was stupid enough to think his name was actually Dr. Yummy."

"You know what your problem is? You're too sweet. Makes you an easy target for practical jokes."

"Apparently."

"Don't beat yourself up about it. We've all done dumb stuff in unfamiliar situations. Besides, I have to admit that Russo is a little yummy if you're into that Norse-god look."

"He's not all that." Emma shrugged. Her initial impression of Dr. Russo was quickly being downgraded from hunk to jerk.

Remembering that David said there were two incidents where Russo had thrown him out of the emergency room, she was curious. "So, what was the second time?"

"The second time?"

"You said Dr. Russo threw you out of the room twice."

"Ah, yeah. The second time I called him a narcissistic prick."

"Are you serious?"

"Sure did. He made this cute little nurse cry, so I laid into him." David smiled and gave her a wink.

"You mean you stuck up for me?"

"Well, it wasn't all about you. He is a narcissistic prick, so it seemed like a great time to remind him of that."

Emma blushed, surprised that a complete stranger would put his own job in jeopardy for her. He must be a good guy, she thought, to stand up to Russo like that.

"I wish you hadn't done that. Gotten into trouble over me."

"Not a big deal." David gave a nonchalant nod. "I'm just that kind of guy."

Though he looked straight ahead, David glanced at her out of the corner of his eye and caught her smiling at him. He stood and extended his hand and smiled. "How 'bout we go on back in now? Chins up, heads held high, like we own the damn place."

She looked at his out-stretched hand and hesitated. Still embarrassed, she dreaded going back inside and facing the staff; even worse having to face Dr. Russo. But she knew she couldn't hide out any longer. David had not only comforted her, he inspired her. She had worked too hard to give up now. No, she would fight. She would go back inside and grovel if needed to keep her job. She accepted his extended hand and pulled herself up and rose from underneath her self-pity and defeat.

"Thank you," she said, "for talking me off my ledge."

She loosened her ponytail then redid it to make sure every hair was in place. She brushed her white skirt to smooth out the wrinkles. Confident she was back together, Emma headed back to the emergency room entrance, her head held defiantly high just the way David had told her.

"Hey, nurse!" He called after her.

She paused in the doorway. Even from that distance she could see the twinkle in his eyes and the way his smile lit up his whole face.

"I didn't catch your name."

"Emma. Emma Paige." She smiled and brushed a strand of hair from her face.

He tipped an invisible hat toward her. "Catch you later, Nurse Paige."

CHAPTER 3

The second day of her orientation Emma arrived not as excited as she would have liked. She sat in her car in the parking garage staring at the clock on her dashboard. It was 6:25 a.m.; 35 minutes before her shift started. Unlike the previous day, Emma dreaded going in. Yesterday she had been excited to begin a new chapter in her life; thrilled at starting her career in nursing. Now, after the way her first day of orientation had ended, she was anxious about what disaster she would have to confront next.

She stared blankly ahead, quietly contemplating whether she had the personality to be a trauma nurse, or if she was perhaps in over her head. There was the possibility she didn't have what it took to work in the high stress environment of the emergency room. During yesterday's trauma she was nervous, her hands were shaking, and she was clumsy. Plus, she looked like a fool thanks to

Kenise's practical joke. She was naïve and gullible; she accepted that fact and questioned if she was too naïve for the job after all.

After Russo ejected her from the trauma room, Emma had recomposed herself with David's encouragement, and she resisted the urge to quit on the spot. When she returned to the Emergency Room expecting the worst. To her surprise, everyone, even Sister Faith, laughed it off. It didn't feel like they were laughing at her but were instead laughing at the circumstances. Apparently, she and Dr. Russo were the only ones who thought calling him Dr. Yummy was a big deal.

Kenise was incredibly apologetic about the matter, insisting she never dreamed Emma believed that the doctor's name was actually Yummy. She took full responsibility for the matter and explained it to both the charge nurse and Sister Faith. As for Dr. Russo she explained that she had played a joke on Emma. He shrugged it off and never addressed the matter with Emma again; he certainly never apologized for his own behavior. Instead, he acted as if nothing had happened and continued to avoid Emma as much as possible.

When the clocked flipped to 6:30 Emma gathered her orientation folder along with her stethoscope and walked to the emergency room entrance. She was reluctant and full of dread, but determined not to reveal her self-doubt. Instead, she hurried to the time clock and offered a warm greeting to everyone she passed along the way. There, she found Kenise along with several nurses gathered round chatting. She smiled as she made her way past them to grab her timecard and prepared to clock-in.

"Oh baby, you can't clock-in yet," Kenise told her. "We can only clock in between 6:38 and 6:52."

"Oh, I didn't know that," she answered.

"Well, you better learn that quick," a rather plump nurse added and laughed with a jiggle. "If you clock-in before 6:38 it counts as overtime and they write you up. Clock in after 6:52 then you're considered late. So, they write you up then too."

"That's right," Kenise agreed. "They don't play around with the time cards here. You can kill a patient and they'll give you a slap on the wrist, but if you're late, they'll send you packing real quick."

"Ain't that the truth," the heavy nurse said. "By the way, I'm Pam. I was off yesterday so I didn't get to meet you yet."

"Emma. It's a pleasure."

"I'm glad you've decided to join us. I've heard so much about you already." Pam replied and all the nurses giggled. "I hear you got the famous Dr. Russo welcome."

"Oh, you heard about that." Emma dropped her head in embarrassment. No doubt the other nurses had a good long laugh at her expense.

"Oh girl, don't worry about that! We've all been on the receiving end of that man's temper." Pam assured her. "That man is like a volcano. Everybody knows he's gonna erupt, we just don't know when and how bad it's going to be."

"That's right, baby," Kenise said. "That's water under the bridge so don't you worry about that another minute. By now, Dr. Russo has forgotten all about it, so you should too."

"He seemed angry enough yesterday, and he didn't even acknowledge my existence the rest of the shift," Emma said. "I'm sure he hates me."

"Girl, he hates everybody," Pam said with a belly laugh. "He's a terrible person. If he wasn't such nice eye candy, the nursing staff would have run him out on a rail years ago."

"He is something pretty isn't he," Kenise said and made everyone giggle and nod their agreement.

Emma gave a shrug and rolled her eyes in response. "I suppose." She was reluctant to offer that man any praise after the way he acted yesterday. Sure, he was remarkably handsome, but he had an ugly disposition and could be downright mean. For a man to catch and hold her attention, he had to be as beautiful on the inside as he was on the outside; like David the paramedic. Dr. Russo just wasn't the same type of sexy as David.

"You suppose?" Kenise scoffed. "Don't act so innocent. I saw how you looked at him, like he was the last piece of fried chicken at the church buffet."

"Well, I have to admit—" Emma started.

"Uh huh, go ahead and say it," Kenise continued to tease her.

"All right, all right. I suppose he does fill out those scrubs rather well. But as pretty as he is on the outside, he seems to be ugly on the inside."

Pam laughed and nodded her agreement. "Who cares about the inside? I'm not looking to marry the man. Have you seen that butt?"

"No, I haven't noticed." Emma blushed.

"Oh baby girl, take a peek," Kenise blurted out. "You could bounce quarters off his rear end it's so round and firm."

Pam saw the time was now 6:52. "Time to clock in ladies."

After they had clocked-in they headed as a group to the main nursing station ready to receive the report from the off-going shift. On the assignment board Emma saw she was again with Kenise for the day which was both a blessing and a curse. Kenise was a very experienced nurse who knew all the policies and was very skilled in-patient care. She was a good mentor to learn the policies from, but she was also a prankster. Emma had learned the hard way not to accept everything Kenise said as fact. She didn't think Kenise would say or do anything that would compromise a patient's care or intentionally get her into trouble; yet, Kenise was a prankster which made Emma rather uncomfortable.

Emma wanted to make certain there was no repeat of the Dr. Yummy episode, so she took a moment to speak to Kenise about it one more time. She didn't want to continue to harp on the topic, only to feel confident that the information Kenise gave her would be accurate, and she would not find herself the punch-line of another joke.

"Kenise, can we speak privately before we start the shift?" Emma asked.

"Oh course, baby. What is it?"

"Well, I wanted to say I'm not mad about yesterday. I should have known you were joking."

"Baby let's forget about that. I shouldn't have teased you."

"Like I said, I take responsibility for being so gullible. I hope you understand how important it is to me that I get everything just right. So, it would be helpful if I knew that I can take you at your word on things around here."

"Oh dear. I'm so sorry that I made you question me like that. I don't want you worrying at all," Kenise insisted. "I'll stick to the facts and save the jokes for later."

"Thank you. I'm very serious about this job and want to do the best I can. It really means a lot to me."

"I'm sure you will be a wonderful nurse," Kenise said. "But honey, let me give you some advice. You need to, unclench your butt cheeks and ease up on yourself. Nursing is a stressful job. Whether you're in the ER, the ICU, or wiping butts on the geriatric floor. It's all stressful and you gotta learn a way to deal with it. If you don't, you're gonna end up going home every night crying into a bottle of vodka."

"That's exactly what David said."

"David? You mean David the paramedic?"

"Yes. He talked me off the ledge yesterday when Dr. Russo threw me out of the trauma room."

"Baby, you watch out for that one. He won't just talk you off the ledge, he'll talk you out of your panties if you're not careful."

Kenise's comment came as a shock. David seemed to be very sincere and caring. He was the only person in the department who had made any attempt to console her, and he had even defended her to Dr. Russo. Why would she need to watch out for someone as kind as David seemed to be?

"But he seemed so sweet," Emma replied.

"Oh, he is. Sweet as honey, that one," Kenise agreed. "He'd give anybody the shirt off his back if they needed it. But he's a player. He's dated half the women in this hospital. They won't even allow him in the unit anymore cause he's such a womanizer."

"Oh my!" That disappointed Emma, but then again, she questioned the source. David seemed like such a nice man; she couldn't believe he was a womanizer. She liked David, but the last thing she wanted was to be the target of his affections. "I'll keep my distance then."

"Well, I didn't mean you should avoid him. He knows his stuff, and he isn't necessarily a bad guy. He's just the typical single man around here; they're all dogs. Just don't let him take advantage of you."

"Right now, I'm not interested in dating anyone anyway. I'm just worried about getting through orientation. I'll worry about everything else when I make it past my 90-day evaluation."

"You'll do just fine. You seem to know your stuff; all you need to do is focus on learning the way we do things around here. And believe me, everybody here wants to see you succeed. Even that nasty Dr. Russo."

It relieved Emma to hear Kenise's encouragement. She believed Kenise was sincere, and it helped her be more confident in her own ability to adapt to her job duties. It was just a matter of finding her way around, learning how things were done and knowing what they expected of her. She felt her confidence growing again. But then she recalled how nervous she was during the trauma the day before and how Dr. Russo had yelled at her.

"I'm not so sure. I know my nursing skills, but I wasn't ready for it to be so stressful and high pressure. I didn't expect my first patient to be so young and in such bad shape. It really made me nervous that I might mess up and cause him… you know, I might do something that could make him worse."

"Well baby girl, what kinda patients did you expect to have in the emergency room? This is a trauma center."

"I expected to see some pretty sad things and a lot of bad accidents. I suppose I just wasn't expecting to have a trauma the first five minutes of work."

"And now you see why some of us folks joke our way through the shift. Girl, I tell ya, if I didn't laugh some days I'd have to cry. And you saw firsthand how far tears get you around here." Kenise waved her hand dramatically as if she were waving goodbye. "Just remember. When you have a really sick patient, let everybody know. Don't be afraid to ask for help. If you have a patient that's crashing, you need to call in the doc, the charge nurse, Respiratory and even housekeeping. Nobody expects you to be working miracles on your own around here. And like you saw yesterday, when there's a trauma, there's a whole slew of people in the room. Nobody will let you make a critical mistake, in fact, part of every trauma team member's job is to double check everybody else. That's why when the doctor orders a drug, one nurse pulls the drug and checks the dose, then a second nurse verifies everything before giving it. We all check each other and watch out for each other. And more important, we watch out for our patients. Believe me baby girl, we watch out for each other. If a mistake happens, and I promise it will, it's not your fault, it's not mine, it's the whole team's mistake."

Emma was glad to see Kenise take such a serious view of teamwork. After the Dr. Yummy incident, Emma had looked at her as a somewhat unreliable source of information. After hearing her talk about teamwork, Emma realized that despite her relaxed nature and jocular attitude, Kenise was a good nurse. She had a good work ethic and cared about the patients and her co-workers.

"I appreciate you telling me that," Emma replied. "That really makes me feel better."

"We are a team and we help each other." Kenise emphasized.

Confident they understood each other, Emma's thoughts returned to the poor trauma victim. She had worried about him, wondering if he had survived and how he was doing.

"Kenise, have you heard what happened to the poor guy from the accident yesterday. Dr. Russo made me leave the room, and I was wondering just what happened. Did he make it?"

"They rushed him to the O.R. I don't know if he survived or not, but most likely, when you have a dissected aorta you bleed out in a matter of minutes, so I don't have a lot of hope there. He made it to surgery so maybe they saved him."

"Oh, that's terrible! He seemed like such a nice guy."

Kenise widened her eyes and pulled her head back in surprise. "Now how can you possibly know that? He could have been a horrible person. He could have been a serial killer as far as we know."

"No, he's a good guy. You can tell a lot about a person buy how they dress and take care of themselves."

"Oh, really?" Kenise placed her hands on both hips and gave Emma a judgmental look. "Then tell me Miss Cleo, how could you possibly know anything about that man by the way he looked? I saw nothing but blood and bruises."

"Well, for one he was clean shaven. And you could smell he wore nice cologne."

"So? He could be a pimp. Pimps and drug dealers wear some real nice smelling cologne too." Kenise laughed. "What else makes you think he's so nice?"

"His clothes were neatly pressed with creases, like he was in the military or in law enforcement."

"Jeffery Dahmer was in the military, too." Kenise pointed out.

"He also had nicely manicured nails and even his toenails were clean and neatly trimmed. Bad men don't have pedicures."

"Didn't that guy in that American Psycho movie wear nice creased shirts and have mani's and pedi's?"

"Well, ok." Emma shrugged in exasperation. "Maybe you're right. He could have been a horrible person, or he could have been a saint. I don't know. I still can't help but feel sorry for him and hope that he's all right."

"I know you mean well, but baby you can't get so emotionally involved in patients like that. You'll end up on 6th floor in a straitjacket if you take all the tragedy on yourself. When there's a patient, you take care of them as best you can. Once they leave this ER, your job is done and you forget about 'em."

"I hear what you're saying," Emma agreed. It would be unhealthy if she got overly involved and emotional about each patient. But she couldn't just mechanically 'load the truck' and detach herself from all caring either. "I know you're right, but I don't think I can be that disconnected."

"It's not being disconnected, baby. It's self-preservation. You do what you can for every patient, then let them go."

Kenise could tell that Emma was not ready to give up her starry-eyed thoughts of saving the world. She remembered when she first became a nurse; she had the same starry-eyed belief she could carry the burden of every patient she treated. It wasn't until she found herself drinking away the despair that she realized she needed to keep a healthy distance between her and the tragedies of others. Kenise decided not to pressure Emma to change her beliefs. Time would teach her that valuable lesson.

"Well, if you must satisfy your curiosity, check the patient census. If he's still in the hospital, he'll be on the patient census. Or you could just ask Dr. Russo. He should know."

Emma looked down the hall at the desk where Dr. Russo was sitting reviewing patient charts. "He hates me."

"He doesn't hate you," Kenise chuckled. "He's just hard to get to know. Go ask him and maybe it'll break the ice between you two."

Emma thought about it and considered that perhaps if she spoke to Dr. Russo outside of a stressful emergency situation it would ease the lingering tension between them.

"I think I will," Emma replied. "Surely he can't yell at me for checking on a patient's status."

She walked to the nursing station and stood across the counter where Dr. Russo was reading. He didn't look up from the chart. She continued to stand quietly, waiting for him to acknowledge her presence, and he continued to ignore her.

Emma cleared her throat to get his attention. Still, he didn't acknowledge her. She was certain he saw her there; he was choosing to ignore her.

"Good morning, Dr. Russo," she finally addressed him.

"Morning," he mumbled and continued to read the patient chart.

"I don't think we were properly introduced. I'm Emma. I just started yesterday."

"You just started your nursing program yesterday?" He still didn't look at her and continued reading. "I didn't know we'd be having student nurses so early in the school year."

"I'm not a student, I'm a new employee. I'll be floating between the Emergency Department and the ICU."

"God help us all." He finally looked at her with his piercing green eyes.

Emma stood motionless, looking back at him. She wanted to run but looking into his eyes made her forget how rude he was being to her. Though his words were demeaning, his eyes betrayed him. Those were not the eyes of a villain and he was not as threatening as he tried to appear. She saw something in his face that hinted at kindness no matter how much he tried to hide behind his unpleasant demeanor. Instead of retreating, she held her ground, certain he was not the horrible person he portrayed himself to be. She held his gaze and looked back at him defiantly.

"I'm sorry you feel that way, but I'm not going anywhere. So, get used to it."

"At least you have some backbone." He almost smiled at her boldness but resisted the urge. "Was there something you needed?"

"I was just wondering what happened to the trauma patient from yesterday. The young MVA. I think his name was Thomas, or Thompson."

"Thompson," he replied. "Despite your best efforts the patient survived. He's in ICU."

"Oh, I'm so glad. Do you think he will be all right?"

"I don't know, I left my Tarot cards at home. What I do know is that he had a dissected aorta and a C.H.I....." Russo paused, fully expecting her to ask what the acronym meant.

"Closed head injury." Emma rolled her eyes in frustration. "I know what it means."

"Good, maybe there is hope for you. Anyway, he's intubated and sedated in the I.C.U.; neurology is going to evaluate him this morning."

"Thank you for the information." Emma began to walk away then turned back to him. "Do you think it would be all right if I went up to check on him later?"

"Actually, I think he is not your patient and no longer any of your business." Russo was abrupt in his response. "But if you must then check with your charge nurse."

"Thank you, doctor." Emma again turned to leave but this time Russo spoke.

"Nurse, if I may be so hopeful as to call you that."

Emma turned back and sneered at him. "Yes, Doctor?"

"Just a piece of advice."

"Yes?"

"It's your uniform." Russo rose to his feet and waved his hand up and down at her to point out the way she was dressed.

Emma was wearing again dressed in a white nursing uniform complete with the skirt, hose, shoes and the nursing cap. It may have seemed old-fashioned to some, but it was still very professional and she liked the way she looked.

"What's wrong with my uniform?"

"You look like a bit player from a 1950s soap opera."

"This is a professional nursing uniform," she protested, "and within the nursing dress code policy."

"And I'm sure it thrilled the sisters up in admin to see you wearing it. But look around, see anybody else dressed like Nurse Betty?"

He didn't have to point it out. Emma knew all the other nurses wore scrubs, and she was the only one who wore the traditional white nursing uniform. She had debated whether to switch to the more casual, and comfortable, scrub outfit, but she liked what she was wearing as did the Sisters in Administration. She saw no reason to buy scrubs when she already had several perfectly good nursing uniforms she had purchased during college. After a few paychecks, she might consider buying some scrubs; but for the time she was perfectly fine as she was.

"You know what the problem with you is?" Russo persisted.

Emma clinched her teeth. Why did everyone think she had some sort of problem they needed to diagnose? "No, I don't. But I'm sure you're about to tell me."

"No, I was just wondering if you knew." He smirked and returned to his seat at the desk.

"I will take your fashion advice into consideration, doctor." She glared at him. How dare he presume to tell her how to dress? "Are there any other words of wisdom you'd like to impart before I take my leave?"

"No, you'll probably be gone in a week, so I don't see a need to waste my time."

Emma whipped around and stormed back down the hallway, grumbling to herself as she went. She found Kenise in one of the empty trauma rooms checking the crash cart.

"Hey, baby girl!" Kenise greeted her, but immediately saw the sour expression on her face. "What's wrong? You look like somebody just kicked your puppy."

Emma grabbed the inventory sheet from the top of the code cart and looked at it for a moment, then she slammed it back on the cart. "I hate that man!"

"Let me guess, Dr. Russo."

"Who else? I don't understand why he has to be so mean. He's despicable!"

"Baby, I'm gonna be up front with you. I overheard him complaining to one of the night shift docs about you during shift change last night."

Emma perked up. She didn't understand why Russo was so rude to her, and if Kenise could offer an insight, she was desperate to hear it. "Complaining about me? What for?"

"He's angry that admin hired a new grad with no experience. He says the doctors will have to worry about teaching you instead of being able to depend on you."

"That's not fair! I've been here two days, and he's already thinking I'm incompetent."

"He doesn't think you're incompetent, he thinks you lack the experience you need to be working in the emergency department. There is a difference. In all fairness, most new nurses start out in general care and once they have their confidence, they go into the critical care areas. So, having a new grad in the ER is not that common."

"What am I supposed to do? Go change bedpans in a nursing home for a few years? What trauma experience is that going to offer me? I've worked hard to get here, and I graduated at the top of my class. What more do I have to do?"

"Prove yourself," Kenise answered. "Every new nurse goes through the same thing. Doesn't matter if she's been in the field for 20 minutes or 20 years; when you start a new position, you have to show people what you can do. Being a new graduate, you have a lot more to prove before the doctors will trust your judgment."

"So how do I fix that? He wants me to have more experience, but how am I supposed to get that experience if I don't start somewhere?"

"I understand. All I can say is that you need to know your stuff. Learn all the policies by heart. Learn where all the equipment is so you don't have to fumble around looking for stuff during an emergency. Make sure you know the trauma protocols. Bottom line, make sure you're ready for anything that comes through that door."

Emma took her advice to heart. The rest of the day, all her free time was spent either reading the policy manuals or in the stock rooms learning the location of all the equipment. She was determined not just to prove herself, but even more importantly, she refused to lose her job.

When it was time for her break, rather than head to the lounge for a coffee, she instead headed back to the equipment room to explore. As she stepped inside, she ran right into David carrying an armful of supplies to restock the ambulance.

"Oh, I'm so sorry," she said and quickly picked up the items he had dropped and handed them back.

"No problem." He gave her a warm smile. "Emma, right?"

"Yes."

"I'm David."

"I remember." She spoke shyly and avoided looking at him directly. She was afraid that if she looked directly at him, she would find herself gazing into the most amazing chocolate brown eyes.

Her attempts to avert her eyes didn't go without notice. David dipped his head so she couldn't help but look at him.

"Something wrong?" He asked and gave a sad frown. "Why are you hiding your face from me?"

"No, not at all."

"Something's up. What's wrong?"

"You're really sweet," Emma finally looked directly at him and saw those smiling eyes sparkling back at her.

"Okay," he said. "Sounds like there's a 'but' coming."

"I don't want to hurt your feelings." She looked down at her shoes and put her hands into her skirt pockets. "I'm just not interested in anything other than a good working relationship."

"Oh, really?"

"Don't misunderstand. You seem like a great guy, but I've heard your reputation."

"My reputation?" David sat his supplies on a nearby cart, then leaned back against the wall and crossed his arms. "Care to enlighten me? What reputation might that be?"

Emma quickly regretted the choice of words. "I'm sorry, I shouldn't have said it that way."

"No, don't clam up now. What exactly have you heard about my reputation?" He continued to grin at her in a way that was very disarming. Clearly, he was more amused than upset.

She looked down at the floor and brushed at her skirt to smooth out the creases, a habit she did whenever she was nervous. "I heard that you have a way with the women around here. Not that there's anything wrong with dating around. I just don't want to be on anybody's to-do list."

"Hey, I like your confidence but I'm just being friendly," David chuckled; not in a mean or condescending way but out of amusement. "You're cute and all but just because a guy is nice to you doesn't mean he's coming on to you."

Realizing she had just made a fool of herself yet again, Emma turned red. She assumed David had been flirting with her when he was just being a nice guy. He was handsome and sweet; she wondered if she was taking her feelings and projecting them onto him.

"I'm so sorry." She blushed. "I'm an idiot."

"I wouldn't go that far. Maybe a little of an ass, but idiot might be too strong of a word."

"Oh God, I'm really sorry." She looked up at him and saw his bright smile again, and the twinkling brown eyes.

"Just to clear up any misgivings, I haven't dated anybody in this hospital despite all the gossip and rumors you've heard to the contrary."

"You haven't?" It surprised Emma. He was single and good looking. How could he not have dated any of the hospital nurses? "But I heard you're not allowed in the ICU because—"

He laughed loudly before she even finished.

Suddenly the door opened and in walked Dr. Russo. He looked surprised to find them together. Realizing how it must appear David and Emma looked more guilty than was necessary.

"Did I interrupt?" Dr. Russo raised an eyebrow.

"Not at all. Just restocking the truck," David replied. He gave Emma a slight wink as he picked up his supplies from off the cart and quickly exited.

Emma turned her back to Russo and began exploring one of the supply carts in silence. After a moment she peeked at him from the corner of her eye. He was squatted down to look on the bottom of a shelf with his back toward her. She was a little surprised he had remained silent rather than seize the opportunity to pick at her again.

As he reached deep into the shelving, Emma looked at his impressively broad shoulders and tapered back. With one hand he swept his long blonde hair behind one ear to reveal his perfectly chiseled jaw line and handsome profile. She tried to turn away, but she couldn't help looking at him. He was a beautiful man. She noticed he even smelled nice. She could detect the faint woody and citrus scent of his cologne. Emma inhaled deeply to take in the aroma. She recognized the fragrance but couldn't quiet remember where.

"I'm sorry if this seems forward, but can I ask what perfume you are wearing?" She asked.

"It's called sweat. I went to the gym before work and didn't have time to shower." He laughed dismissively.

"Sorry I asked." She sneered at his narcissistic response.

Having found the supplies he was looking for, Russo stood back up and faced her. "Is there something I can help you find?"

"No, thank you," she turned away and once again began sifting through the supplies. "I'm on break so I thought I'd take a moment to familiarize myself with the supply carts."

"Well, I'm impressed."

He opened the door and started out, then hesitated. "I'm doing an arm cast in Exam #9. Have you ever done one?"

"I've assisted on several during my clinicals."

"Good." He handed her the cast supplies he had in his arms. "I need to put a cast on a patient until he can follow up with a knuckle dragger on Monday."

"Knuckle dragger? You mean an orthopedic?"

"Yep. Knuckle dragger. Bone cracker. Bone Jock. Orthopod, you know the ones; strong as a bull, half as smart."

She laughed as she gathered the supplies in her arms. He had always been so serious and unpleasant to her; it was nice to see him finally smile and crack a joke.

"Why not use a splint?" She quickly clarified her question as not to insult him and incur his wrath. "I'm not questioning your judgment, just wanting to learn. Wouldn't it be better to use a temporary splint and allow for the swelling to go down before following up with an ortho?"

"Good observation. A splint would be best if there's swelling; then I'd wait and put on the cast in a day or two after the swelling has subsided. Unfortunately, this guy is a member of the young invincibles; you know the type, daredevils who think they're too young to die and have no medical insurance. The fracture happened two days ago and rather that seeing a doctor he used an ace bandage to splint it. The swelling has already gone down, and there's no way this kid is going to follow up with ortho. If I don't cast him now, he probably won't get one. He'll just keep it taped up and let it heal crooked."

"That's actually very kind of you," Emma said. She was impressed that Russo would be so vigilant and compassionate that he would place a cast rather than send the patient home knowing he wouldn't have follow-up care. It really didn't make her like Dr. Russo anymore, but at least she could see that he was a conscientious doctor.

"You sound surprised."

"Well, I am actually. You don't seem to be—" she hesitated.

"Nice? Sympathetic?"

"I was going to say, human." Emma took advantage of his kind mood and attempted a joke.

"You may think I'm a rotten person, and maybe I am. But the reason I'm stringent with the staff is because I care about my patients. I didn't become a doctor for the money, if I had I would have been a podiatrist or dermatologist rather than an ER doc."

He handed her a couple more items and then headed back out the door. He paused a moment to hold it open for her.

"I understand," she replied. "That's exactly why I want to be an ER nurse. If it was about money, I would have taken a job in a private practice and have every weekend and holiday off. This is where I want to be. I want to help people."

"Glad to hear that. But don't just tell me, show me you have a fire in you. Do that, and we'll get along fine."

She brushed past him as he held the door, and again she caught the subtle yet sophisticated scent of spicy citrus. *Bleu de Chanel*, she suddenly recognized the aroma. It was the same fragrance she had bought for

Brock on one of his birthdays. She loved the
aroma but unfortunately Brock wasn't a cologne
wearing type of guy.

CHAPTER 4

By the end of her first week of orientation Emma had already become somewhat comfortable with the emergency department routine. She was learning her way around and proving herself to be a fast, and highly motivated, learner. Even Dr. Russo seemed to be easing up on her, although he was still not comfortable with her when it came to the critical patients. At times, he would specifically seek her out, usually for her assistance with some non-urgent procedure such as suturing, starting IV's, and providing discharge instructions. However, his favorite task for Emma was to give patient enemas. Whenever they had a patient with stomach discomfort, Russo would write an order specifically saying, "Have Nurse Emma give the patient an enema." She assumed that was his way of keeping her humble.

The other nurses assured her that Dr. Russo would eventually come around; she just needed to be patient and prove herself to him. Begrudgingly, Emma accepted that she needed to earn his respect. Still she resented it. After all, she had completed nursing school and passed the boards, that should be enough to prove her qualifications. At least that was what she thought. However, she was about to learn the hard way that book knowledge doesn't necessarily equate to good judgment and sound clinical skills.

It was mid-afternoon on Friday, just a few hours before the end of her last shift of the week, when Mrs. Norma Greene arrived in the emergency room. It was a busy afternoon, which was typical for a Friday. The entire staff was occupied with patients when David and his fellow paramedics came pushing Mrs. Greene through the doors on a stretcher.

"Hey sweets," David greeted Emma. "What room do we have for this lovely young lady?"

David's jovial attitude brought a smile to both Mrs. Greene and Emma. He knew how to flatter the ladies.

"Exam seven is open," Emma said and she her smile made it difficult to disguise her pleasure at seeing him again.

David and the other paramedic pushed the stretcher down the hallway as Emma followed. Once they were parked in the room and the patient was connected to the monitor, David gave Emma report.

"This is the fabulous Mrs. Norma Greene. She is 82 years young."

"Oh, you're so incorrigible." Norma laughed and as she did, she began a serious of rumbling coughs.

"As you can hear, Miss Norma has some congested heart failure and has missed her medications for a few days, including her diuretics, so she has some extra fluid on board."

"I ran out a couple days ago and I don't drive, so I couldn't get to the pharmacy," Norma explained.

"Do you live alone?" Emma asked.

"I live with my husband."

"And he doesn't drive?"

"No honey, we haven't driven in years."

David patted Mrs. Greene gently on the shoulder. "Mr. Greene is 86 and has dementia, so she has a lot on her plate. She takes care of her husband but forgets about taking care of herself."

"It's not a burden," Norma clarified. "I've been with my Joe for nearly 65 years. We've always taken care of each other; I can't stop now that he's old."

"Sixty-five years! Congratulations." Emma was genuinely happy for Norma and Joe. She hoped that one day she could find a love that would last as long. "Is someone with your husband right now?"

"My neighbor. She's been such a god-send for us."

"That's good. So, tell me what brings you in today?"

"Well, dear. It's like that handsome boy just said." She gave David a big smile like he was her own son or grandson.

Emma chuckled lightly when Mrs. Greene referred to David as 'that handsome boy'. He was undoubtedly handsome but also, he was far from being a boy. She supposed that when you reach your 80s, most people seem to be young boys or girls.

"I heard him," Emma patted the old woman's hand light. "But it's important that you tell me what's going on in your own words. Just to make sure we're all on the same page."

"Well, honey, I've had congested heart failure for years now. They give me fluid pills and heart medicine, and a few other things I don't know what they are." She waved her hand through the air as she was dismissing the entire thing. "You know doctors today.

They give you pills for this and that, and then more pills to take care of the side effects from the pills they gave you in the first place. Before you know it, you're swallowing half a dozen pills and don't know what for."

"I hear that." Norma wasn't the first patient she met that was on too many pills to remember. "Are you having any chest pain at all?"

"No, honey, I don't have any chest pain. Just short of breath."

Emma took a moment to write notes. Since the patient's chart had not yet arrived, she resorted to the universal nurses document sheet, a paper towel she pulled from the dispenser at the sink.

"And you ran out of your medicines?" She continued her interview.

"Honey, I ran out a couple days ago," she shook her head with in a mixture of disgust and embarrassment. "My daughter usually comes to take me to the store and to the pharmacy, but I guess she just got busy and forgot. I hated to call and bother her since she's got a houseful of grandkids she's minding. I didn't think it would be a problem to miss a few days, so I didn't bother her. I figured she come when she came. But this morning I had such a hard time breathing I had to call the rescue squad."

Emma examined Norma's ankles and pressed the skin to access the edema. They were both swollen and thick with edema. Then she moved to the calves and inspected them. "You have a lot of fluid, you shouldn't miss your medications."

"I gave her a good talking too about that," David said and gave the old lady a stern look. "Next time, Miss Norma is going to call me before she runs out of meds, and I'll pick them up for her."

"Well, that's sweet of you," Emma smiled at him. It was no surprise that David would offer to do such a kind gesture for a stranger. He had already proven himself to be a kind man with a big heart.

"We go back a long way," David explained. "Miss Norma was my first call when I became a paramedic. We've met up every couple of months since."

"That's right, he's been my personal angel for a few years now. Norma reached out and grabbed his hand and patted it affectionately then let go again. "And he's awfully pretty to look at too."

"That he is," Emma said before realizing she had spoken. She looked at David and blushed slightly. "I mean he really is a good man."

"The best," David said and gave a wink.

Emma redirected her attention back to assessing the patient. "Ok Mrs. Greene…"

"Honey, you can just call me Norma. I don't mind."

"All right Norma, I need to listen to your lungs. Can you take some deep breaths?"

Emma placed her stethoscope on Norma's chest and listened intently, moving the bell of the stethoscope from one side to the other. Then she placed the bell over the heart, "Breathe normally," she instructed while she continued to listen and watch the heart tracing on the cardiac monitor.

"You have a lot of fluid in your lungs, but your heart sounds good and your pulse oximetry is 95%." Emma took Norma's wrist to feel her pulse while continuing to question her. "Does the oxygen seem to help with the shortness of breath?"

Again, Norma made a horrendous rattling cough. "Yes honey, it's starting to help. I just feel so congested. If I could just cough some of this up, I think I'd feel better."

"I'll talk to Dr. Russo about getting you some respiratory treatments and some diuretics. I believe you'll feel a lot better after you void some of that excess fluid."

"All right, dear. Thank you."

David took Mrs. Greene by the hand and gave her a reassuring pat. "I need to go now. You're in good hands with Emma."

Norma squeezed his hand and smiled at the two paramedics. "You boys are so good to me. I don't know what I'd have done if it wasn't for you."

"Our pleasure, Miss Norma," David said.

The two men headed out into the hallway followed by Emma. Outside the trauma room David handed Emma his clipboard with the patient's ambulance charting. "If you'll sign off on the transfer sheet then we'll be out of here."

Emma took his clipboard and signed the paper. Then, David passed the clipboard to the other paramedic. "You go ahead, I'll be there in a minute."

His partner gave David a grin then headed down the hallway.

David leaned closer to Emma and spoke softly so that no one would overhear. "Do me a favor. When Miss Norma is ready for discharge, give me a shout over the radio and we'll circle around and take her back home. She doesn't have anybody to come and pick her up and I don't want her to have to call for a taxi."

"That' so sweet of you," Emma answered.

"Just keep it under your hat, I don't want her to get billed for it. Miss Norma's a good lady and really doesn't have anybody she can depend on. Her one daughter is MIA all the time. Usually we get a call for Mr. Greene, but now she's going downhill too. I just want to make sure she gets home okay and has what she needs."

"Of course. We'll get her all fixed up and I'll give you a call when she's ready for discharge."

"Don't tell anybody," David whispered. "I don't want people to think me and Miss Norma have something on the down-low. You know how people talk around here."

Emma laughed lightly. "You're a good man. She should be so lucky."

Emma watched as he headed down the hall. In the short time she had known David, she already liked him; a lot actually. She hadn't met too many men with such a big heart. He genuinely cared for people; not just his patients, but for people in general. She smiled as she watched him leave, admiring how confidently he sauntered down the hallway, happily smiling and greeting everyone he passed.

It wasn't until David had passed though the automatic doorways and was out of sight that she turned down the hallway in search of Dr. Russo. When she found him, he was in the dictation room, intently studying an x-ray on the computer screen. She stood there quietly waiting to be acknowledged, knowing full well he saw her. He knew she was in the doorway; he could see her out of the corner of his eye, but he still refused to look at her until it was unavoidable. She politely and patiently waited, fuming inside the whole time.

As Emma stood there, tapping her foot in frustration, the scent of his cologne greeted her. It wasn't an overpowering aroma, rather it was like a whisper that ever so softly taunted her sense of smell. She savored the sensuality of his fragrance, which made the wait a little more tolerable. After another moment, she surrendered and audibly cleared her throat to get his attention.

"Yes?" He continued looking at the computer screen.

"I'm sorry to bother you, but we have a new admit in room seven. 82-year-old white female with a history of chronic CHF. The patient arrived via ambulance with shortness of breath. She reported she has missed her diuretics for the last two days."

"What's her vitals?"

"Sinus rhythm at 70. Respirations 20. She's on 2 liters of O2 and oximetry is 95%. She has rales throughout and complains of moderate shortness of breath. She has bilateral pitting edema in lower extremities."

"So, Nurse Paige. What do you suggest?" Dr. Russo turned and looked at her for the first time.

She hated when he tested her, which seemed to be all the time. Then again, she liked to prove her knowledge to him. She knew that with each correct answer she was closer to the day he would have confidence in her and show her the respect she deserved.

"I'd suggest that we insert a Foley catheter to measure output and then treat her with Lasix and breathing treatments." She responded confidently.

"Almost right."

"Oh? What did I miss?" She was sure that Lasix was the proper treatment along with monitoring urine output, and aerosol treatments would help with the patient's breathing.

"For one thing, Respiratory is going to jump down your throat if you ask them to give breathing treatments to a patient with CHF."

"But she's short of breath." Emma didn't see why it was wrong to give a patient breathing medication to relieve shortness of breath.

"Why does she have dyspnea?" Russo continued to press.

"Because of the excess fluid." Emma sighed. The answer had been obvious. The breathing treatment wouldn't be indicated because the underlying cause of the shortness of breath was the fluid. The patient needed diuretics not a bronchodilator.

"I understand now, " Emma said. "So, I would recommend that we do a Foley catheter and IV Lasix, and not the respiratory treatments."

"Almost right."

Emma raised her eyebrows, unsure of what she had said wrong.

"You said, 'we should insert a Foley'." His eyes narrowed slightly, and he gave a half-smile. "The correct answer is that you, not we, should insert a Foley. We, or more precisely, I, do not insert urine catheters."

"Of course, Doctor." She gave a soft sigh of relief, pleased that he would make a joke and smile at her rather than offer his usual biting criticism.

"Very good. Go ahead and put in the catheter, then give 40 mg IV Lasix. Make sure you check for drug allergies beforehand."

"Yes, doctor."

Back in the patient's room Emma had finished inserting the catheter and was pulling up 40 mg of Lasix into a syringe. She took a moment then checked the patient's armband. "Norma, can you tell me your full name, please?"

"Norma Jean Greene."

"And your date of birth?"

"October 15th, 1929."

Emma confirmed the information Norma provided with what was on the patient armband. Satisfied that all was well. She looked at the second armband that was a bright red color. This band listed the patient's drug allergies.

"Mrs. Greene, according to the allergy alert armband you're allergic to Bactrim, is that correct?"

"Yes, honey I believe that's what it is."

"Do you have any other allergies?"

"I think the doctor said…" she paused and tried to remember exactly what medication she was allergic to. "I think it's sulfur, does that sound right?"

"Sulfa? Bactrim is a sulfa drug, so that makes sense," Emma noted. "Any other allergies you know of?"

"No, honey. Not that I know of."

"Have you had Lasix before? Or Furosemide?"

"I don't remember. Lasix sounds familiar, but I can't be sure. I've had to take so many different drugs lately, and then my husband's medications. I'm forgetful and it all starts to run together."

"I understand. Dr. Russo has asked me to give you a medication called Lasix. It's a diuretic. It will help get some of this fluid off so you can breathe better," Emma explained. She injected the medication into the IV port then followed with a syringe of saline flush. "In the next few minutes you will probably feel like you have to urinate. Remember, you have a catheter in, so just relax and let nature take its course."

"Okay, honey." Norma replied and began to fan herself with her hand. "Would you turn the air on a little bit, it's awfully hot in here."

"Sure." The room didn't feel hot to her, in fact, it seemed a little cool. Emma checked the thermostat; it was set at 68 degrees. She lifted the cover and turned the temperature down to 65. "It'll take a couple minutes for the air to kick on."

"I don't feel right," Norma complained in a weak voice.

Emma returned to the bedside and could see that Norma was sweating profusely. Her hands felt cold and clammy, and her face had become extremely pale. Suddenly, the heart monitor alarmed. Emma looked up and saw Norma's heart rate was now 130 and climbing.

"Mrs. Greene? Do you feel okay?"

Norma did not respond. Emma shook her gently by the shoulders but there was still no response.

Emma felt light-headed and on the verge of panicking. She took a deep breath to gather her wits then she reacted. She quickly pressed the code blue button on the wall above the patient bed; immediately the overhead alarm followed by an announcement over the PA system, "Code Blue. Emergency Department. Trauma Room Four."

Within seconds Emma had lowered the head of the stretcher so that the patient was lying flat, then she grabbed the crash cart from the corner of the room and pulled it to the bedside. Dr. Russo rushed in followed by the charge nurse, Pam, and several other nurses and the pharmacist.

"What do we have?" Dr. Russo asked urgently and immediately began to assess the patient.

"The patient was admitted with edema and congestive heart failure. This is the lady I spoke to you about earlier. I gave her 40 mg Lasix IV. She immediately began complaining that she felt hot. She became diaphoretic and then unresponsive." Emma explained.

Dr. Russo watched the monitor and placed two fingers on the side of Norma's throat. "She has a pulse, it's pretty weak. Let's get her in Trendelenburg and somebody get a pressure."

Quickly, Emma adjusted the stretcher to Trendelenburg position with the head of the bed tilted downward and her feet were elevated. She then placed a blood pressure cuff around Mrs. Greene's arm and pressed the BP button on the heart monitor to start the measurement.

Dr. Russo examined the red armband that was taped around the patient's wrist. "She's allergic to Bactrim?"

"Yes, doctor." Emma answered.

"And you gave her Lasix?" Russo raised his voice.

"Was that not right?" Emma stammered.

"You don't give Lasix to a patient who's allergic to Bactrim. Bactrim is a sulfa-class antibiotic."

"Oh my God! She's allergic to Lasix." Her heart felt like it was in her throat. She suddenly realized her mistake. Lasix contains a sulfa component so if a patient is allergic to Bactrim, there is a high likelihood they will also be allergic to Lasix.

"Really? What gave that away?" Dr. Russo glared at her. "She's having an anaphylactic reaction. She needs epinephrine now!"

With trembling hands and tears streaming down her face, Emma pulled the box of epinephrine from the cart, and prepared to inject the syringe into the IV port.

"What the hell are you doing?" Russo grabbed the syringe out of Emma's hand. "You're about to give a cardiac dose! Are you determined to kill this poor woman?"

Emma was frightened and frustrated. She wasn't upset that Dr. Russo was yelling at her again; what bothered her was that she had made such a mistake. She was horrified at the thought that she had given this sweet woman the wrong medication and may have killed her.

Pam rushed to the bed and gently moved Emma aside. "I've got this," she said.

Hesitantly Emma backed away as Pam took her place assisting Dr. Russo. She felt horrible. The pain and guilt of her error was too much. She ran from the room, down the hallway and out the ambulance doors; crying hysterically as she went. Once outside she continued to run. She ran past the ambulances, through the patient parking lot, into the employee parking lot. She didn't stop until she reached her old Volkswagen bug.

Emma fully intended to leave and not look back. There was no way she wouldn't be fired after such a horrible mistake, and even if she wasn't, she couldn't face the possibility of harming another patient.

When she arrived at her vehicle, she realized she had left her keys and purse in her locker in the nurses' lounge. Breathing heavily from running, she collapsed to her knees at the side of her car and cried hysterically. She didn't want to go back inside; she wanted to just go home. After all, not only did she expect to lose her job, she fully expected to lose her nursing license as well. So why should she bother going back except for the need to retrieve her keys and purse?

She forced herself to get up from off her knees and then sat on the curb next to her car. She buried her face in her hands, horrified at her own bad judgment. Poor Miss Norma had trusted her and depended on her, and she had failed her. She failed as a nurse and may have caused someone's death. It was not the fear of losing her job that tortured her, but the guilt of causing harm to poor Mrs. Greene.

"Hey," a familiar voice distracted her from his sorrow.

She recognized that voice; it was David. He always seemed to turn up whenever she was at her lowest, like a guardian angel. This time she didn't want to be comforted but wanted to be left alone to suffer with her guilt. She lowered her head again and did not look at him.

"What's wrong?" He asked and squatted down beside her.

Emma crossed her arms and hugged her knees to her in almost an upright fetal position. She looked like a lost little girl.

"Emma? What's wrong? It can't be all that bad." David persisted and sat on the curb next to her. He remained patiently quiet, waiting for her to speak when she was ready.

"It's… it's… Mrs. Greene." She finally stammered between her sobs.

"Norma? What about her?".

"I'm a murderer." She broke into sobbing again. "I accidently gave her the wrong medicine, and she went into shock."

"Oh, no!" He had a sincere affection for Mrs. Greene, and it saddened him to hear the news. "Poor Miss Norma! Did she expire?"

"I don't know. She went into anaphylactic shock and coded. She was alive when I ran out, but I don't know."

Emma turned to David and rested her head on his shoulder. "I screwed up, David. Really bad. What if I killed her?"

The news was a blow to him emotionally, but he maintained his composure. Though he had a great fondness for Mrs. Greene, he could see how distraught Emma was over the incident. There was nothing he could do for Mrs. Greene at that moment, so he would focus on comforting Emma. He wrapped his arm around her shoulder to comfort her. "So, you don't know if she's passed or not?"

"No… I don't know for sure."

David took his phone from his pocket and pushed the direct connect button and spoke into the phone. "Hey Rick, you still in the ER?"

A moment later Rick's voice responded on the other end. "Affirmative."

"Can you check on Mrs. Greene for me? She's the little old lady with CHF we brought in earlier."

"Already on it," Rick responded. "There was a code called, but she wasn't in full arrest. Her pressure bottomed out from a reaction to Lasix. She's stable now and on an epi drip."

"Thanks man!" David said. "I'm out-of-pocket for five or ten minutes so shout if we get a call."

"Will do."

David slid the phone back into his pocket and sighed with relief. "See, you're not a murderer. At least not a very good one."

Emma wiped the tears from her cheeks, then finally looked at him. Her eyes were puffy and bloodshot, and her hair was in disarray.

"You look like a mess." David laughed and gently swept the hair out of her face.

"I really screwed up."

"People make mistakes. The best thing you can do is to learn from it. I can guarantee you'll never make the same mistake again."

"I can't go back in there! They're going to fire me over this."

"Honestly, I don't know what's going to happen. You might get fired; you might not. One thing I do know, if you want to be a nurse, you can't do it out here in the parking deck. You need to go back inside and face the music, otherwise you're just throwing in the towel."

David rose to his feet and extended his hand to Emma. "Come on."

Hesitantly she took his hand and stood up. She smoothed out the wrinkles in her nursing skirt and tidied her uniform. David placed a hand gently on Emma's cheek and looked into her eyes. "You'll be all right," he assured her. "No matter what happens, you'll survive. I promise."

Emma looked into his sparkling brown eyes and she drew strength from his gaze. For some reason she believed him. If she lost her job, she would land on her feet and survive. Spontaneously, Emma stood on her tip-toes and pressed her lips to his. She kissed him deeply. Instinctively, he responded and wrapped her in his strong arms and held her tightly. Just as quickly, David released her and stepped back. His expression was that of embarrassment and shock.

"I'm sorry," he said and took another step back.

"No, it was me. I shouldn't have…" Emma's face became flushed. She backed away and without another word she turned and ran back toward the emergency room parking lot.

The kiss surprised David; not just that she would kiss him but by his own response to her advance. He laughed lightly to himself and shook his head. "What a dame," he said aloud using his Humphrey Bogart impression.

Once she was a within sight of the emergency room entrance Emma slowed to a normal walk. She touched her hand slightly to her lips and managed a smile, remembering the taste of David's mouth and the soft texture of his lips. As the automatic doors opened, she paused for a moment and took a long deep breath. She checked her uniform again and smoothed out her skirt. Then with her head held high she marched back inside.

She entered the emergency department ready to face the humiliation and the inevitable verbal assault by Dr. Russo. She expected to find Sister Faith waiting to deliver her termination papers. Instead, the department was busy as a beehive with nurses running between patient rooms, phones ringing, and work proceeding as normal. There was little notice given to her as she walked down the hallway toward the nursing station. When she rounded the corner, she came face to face with Pam.

"Girl, where'd you go?" She barked in a hurried tone. "There's a 400-pound chocolate hostage waiting for you in trauma 10."

"Chocolate hostage?" Emma asked. That was a medical slang term she had yet heard.

"Think about it, girl." Pam smirked. "Dr. Russo specifically wrote in his order and I will quote," she picked up a patient clipboard and read the order aloud. "Please have Nurse Paige give the patient a large volume enema. Repeat every thirty minutes times three until patient has a bowel movement. Unquote."

"I guess that means I'm back in purgatory." Emma remarked.

"You might be there for a while. He's actually referring to you as Nurse Enema now."

"Go figure. He's just a schoolyard bully, after all."

Emma wasn't surprised that Russo had progressed to name calling, but she was surprised to be assigned another patient as if nothing had happened.

"What about Mrs. Greene? Is she all right?" Emma asked.

"We transferred her to observation. If all goes well, she'll be released in 6 hours and not have to spend the night."

"Thank God."

"Thank him after you deal with that beached whale," Pam said and handed her the patient's chart. "She hasn't taken a dump in days and is in there crying like one of those howler monkeys on Discovery Channel."

Emma decided not to question or press her luck with the Mrs. Greene medication error. She had no doubt that later she would face the repercussions, but at least for now, she still had her job.

In room 10 where Emma found her patient, an obese 40-year-old Caucasian woman holding her abdomen and pacing the floor. Emma was grateful to see that the woman wasn't quite the 400 pounds Pam had reported. She was definitely obese, maybe 250 pounds but not as large as she had been led to believe.

"Ms. Susan Jordan?" Emma asked as she entered the room.

"Oh. Oh! Heeeeeelp!" Susan grabbed at her stomach with both hands and bent over in pain. "I need a laxative or an enema. Please, something for the pain."

"We have to hold off on pain medicine for the moment. If you're constipated the pain medicine might make it worse."

"It can't get any worse," she screamed as another wave of pain hit. "You've got to do something. I can't take this."

"The doctor has asked me to give you an enema."

"An enema!" She yelled at Emma. "I could have given myself an enema at home!"

"Ma'am, just try to keep calm."

"Oh God! Oh God! Oh God!" The woman clutched her stomach again and bent over in pain. "It feels like I've got a bowling ball stuck down there binding me up. Please! Give me a laxative or something. Stick a crow bar up there and take it out, I don't care what you've got to do. Just do something for the pain. I'm begging you, please!"

"Okay, Miss Jordan, let's get you back on the stretcher," Emma said, and she aided the lady back onto the table. "Were you having this much discomfort when the doctor examined you?"

It concerned Emma that the patient was having such painful cramping, and that it happened in waves. By her behavior, there was no reason to suspect that the woman was exaggerating or faking her pain to get narcotics. She hated to do it, but she wondered if she should call Dr. Russo back in the room to examine the patient again. Surely, he was not aware of how much pain the woman was in.

"It wasn't this bad. It's gotten a lot worse in the past few minutes," Ms. Jordan groaned.

"Miss Jordan, if it's all right I want to check your abdomen for a moment." Emma closed the curtain and began to palpitate the stomach, pressing gently over differing locations. "Tell me if you feel any discomfort."

"Right there." Miss Jordan groaned in pain as Emma pressed over the lower mid-abdomen.

"Miss. Jordan, when was your last menstrual period?" Emma inquired.

"I don't remember. My monthlies have always been irregular. Oh, Jesus, Jesus Jesus!" She suddenly cried out as another wave of pain hit. "Just give me the enema. I can't take this. Just do it. Do it!"

"I'll get the enema kit ready, but I think we need to have Dr. Russo come back to examine you again. You seem to be significantly obstructed; we may need to do a manual dis-impaction."

Emma pressed the call button.

"Can I help you," a voice asked over the speaker.

"I need Dr. Russo please," Emma said.

"I'll let him know."

"I think it's coming out! Arrrrrgggggghhhh!" Ms. Jordan cried out and grunted.

Emma stood beside the stretcher and lifted the patient's gown. Just as she did, Dr. Russo entered the room.

"What's the problem?" He demanded. "Do you not know how to give an enema?"

"Oh, lord!" Emma gasped as she looked under the patient's gown. "She's crowning."

"What?" Russo hurried around to the side of the bed.

To his surprise, he saw the top of a baby's head protruding from between the patient's thighs. "You didn't tell us you're pregnant!"

"Pregnant?! I'm not pregnant!" Miss Jordan protested.

"I think I have to disagree with you, Ms. Jordan! That is definitely a baby's head sticking out of your vagina." Dr. Russo said with a touch of hysteria and amusement. He quickly pulled on a pair of rubber gloves and positioned himself at the foot of the bed.

"Emma. Call L&D. Tell them to get a team down here stat."

Emma had been standing frozen in place with her mouth open and staring in disbelief at the top of the baby's head. She shook herself, then hit the call button on the wall so hard she broke it.

"Can I help you?" the voice asked over the speaker.

"We need Labor and Delivery stat, please. And tell them they need to be here like 5 minutes ago."

"Got it," the voice replied.

"Miss Jordan, I need you to bend your knees up and open your legs wide," Russo instructed.

"But I'm not pregnant!" Miss Jordan insisted again but did as the doctor instructed. "This can't be happening."

"Ma'am, I need you to push," Dr. Russo said. "Push hard like you're having a bowel movement."

"You need to take deep breaths in and out," Emma coached and panted with her. "Fast and deep. Fast and deep. Like you've been running!"

Ms. Jordan pushed and groaned loudly. A moment later the baby's shoulders were out, and with another push the entire infant was in

Russo's hands. It moved only slightly but was otherwise limp and motionless.

"You've got a little boy!" Russo announced proudly.

"I need two sets of hemostats and scissors," Russo turned to Emma. He was surprised to find she was already handing him two umbilical cord clamps and a pair of surgical scissors. He gave her a surprised look.

"The benefits of knowing where everything is," Emma grinned back. At that moment she was grateful for the time she spent reviewing the contents of every drawer, bin and cabinet in the department. Because of her efforts, she knew exactly where to look and didn't need to waste time fumbling around for equipment.

Russo took the clamps and clipped them onto the umbilical cord. Once both clamps were in place, he handed the scissors back to Emma. "Since dad's not here, I see no reason you shouldn't do the honors."

Emma hesitated only a moment, then took the scissors and cut the umbilical cord between the two clamps. Dr. Russo stimulated the baby by rubbing its back and immediately the infant began to cry. Its color quickly changed from gray to bright pink and the baby kicked his feet and waved his arms vigorously.

Emma found a couple of clean towels on the nearby linen cabinet and handed them to Russo. He used one to dry the fluid from the baby then wrapped the infant snuggly in the second towel before laying the baby gently in the mother's arms.

"Trouble seems to follow you," he said and gave Emma a smile. Her calm demeanor and her quick thinking in the situation impressed him. Had Emma not been alert, the delivery could have been disastrous.

"I guess I'm a magnet for trouble." She couldn't help but smile brightly. Not only was she thrilled at seeing a baby being born, but she was also relieved that for the first time Dr. Russo had treated her with kindness and appreciation.

"Oh my God!" The woman suddenly screamed loudly.   "Something's   wrong!   There's something else there."

"You're   all   right,"   Russo   reassured her.   "It's   just   the   placenta   being delivered."

Russo resumed his position at the foot of the bed. "Nurse Emma is going to hold the baby for a few moments. Once the placenta is out, you can have him back."

Emma took the infant from the mother and held it in her arms and bounced it lightly.

Russo continued to work as the mother pushed out the placenta, but he could not help but glance over at Emma. She cradled the new born snuggly in her arms, her white uniform stained with spots of blood and amniotic fluid. In that moment, Dr. Russo saw her as if for the first time. Despite her mistakes, her short-comings and her insecurities, Emma had the heart of a nurse. As he watched her cooing lovingly at the baby and rocking it in her arms, for the first time he saw her as a woman.

CHAPTER 5

Emma awoke to the warm sun shining on her face and the sound of birds chirping outside her bedroom window. She yawned and stretched her arms overhead, then pulled the covers back over her and rolled onto her side. She looked at the clock on her nightstand; the time was 8:15 a.m. She closed her eyes and snuggled under the warm blanket.

"Oh my god!" She blurted out and jumped up in bed. "It's 8:15!"

She should have been at work almost two hours ago! Had she forgotten to set the alarm or was she just so tired that she had slept through it? She yanked one of her nursing uniforms off the hanger in her closet then hurried to the bathroom. She turned on the shower then went back to get her phone from her nightstand. She thought she had better call the hospital and let them know she had overslept.

When she looked at her phone, she saw that it was Saturday. She sighed in relief since she had the weekend off. It had been a long week of orientation and her brain was taxed with all the new policies and information she had absorbed over the week. She was mentally exhausted from the constant sparring with Dr. Russo, and she was still upset over the incident with Mrs. Greene and the Lasix. It was no wonder she had slept late and awoke in a state of confusion.

She walked back and turned the shower off, deciding she could do with a cup of black coffee instead. In the kitchen she found Jennifer was sitting cross-legged in a chair eating cereal.

"Morning, hon," Jennifer said.

"Morning." Emma shuffled to the coffeemaker and poured herself a cup.

"You look like you've had a rough night."

"I tossed and turned all night long." Emma yawned and sipped at her coffee. "I heard monitor beeps and code blue alarms in my sleep all night long. And then there was Dr. Russo yelling."

"Who's Dr. Russo?"

"You remember, I told you about him treating me like a student."

"Oh, Dr. Yummy." Jennifer laughed.

"Please don't remind me."

"Sorry. But I thought he was starting to be nice to you."

"It depends on the day and the moment. One minute he's taking time out to teach me something, then the next he's yelling at me for not moving fast enough to suit him. I can't seem to win."

"I'm sure he'll come around in time."

Emma sat down at the table across from Jennifer and sipped at her coffee. Chase, Jennifer's boyfriend appeared, walked into the kitchen having just gotten out of the shower. He was completely naked, except for a towel he was using to dry his hair as he walked into the room.

"Chase!" Emma squealed and covered her eyes. "Oh my God!"

"Sorry, sorry." He was laughing as he quickly wrapped the towel around his waist. "I didn't know you were here."

"I live here! Where else would I be?" Emma peeked from between her fingers to see if Chase had covered himself. Satisfied that he was at least half-way decent she went back to drinking her coffee.

"I thought you may have gone to work," Chase answered. "Or you'd hooked up with somebody last night and stayed out."

"I don't hook up!"

"You know what your problem is?" Chase asked.

Oh, there it was. Emma closed her eyes tightly in an attempt not to fly into a fit of rage. Just what she needed; another man telling her what her problem is.

"You need to get laid," Chase said.

"Maybe you should, Em," Jennifer said. "It'd do you some good to get laid."

"I'm not interested in one-night stands."

"Obviously," Chase observed. "When's the last time you had a date? Or even gone out other than to the library or work?"

"My social life is not up for discussion, Chase. Why don't you go put some clothes on and mind your own business?"

"Fine." He turned and headed back toward the bedroom; as he did, he untucked the towel from around his waist and let it fall to the floor behind him, revealing his naked butt.

"Chase!" Emma shouted at him and both girls started laughing.

"You know, he's only trying to be helpful," Jennifer said after he disappeared back into their bedroom.

"By showing me his ass?"

"You know what I mean," Jennifer answered. "We both think you need to start dating again."

"I'm not ready."

Jennifer reached across the table and placed her hand on Emma's. "Em, honey. It's been four years. You need to move on with your life. Seriously. It's time. No, it's past time."

"I just graduated college and started a new job. Now's not the right time. And, just because I'm not dating anyone doesn't mean anything. I haven't met the right man yet."

"Unless Mr. Right is the UPS man or the pizza delivery man I doubt he's gonna come knocking on the door. You have to put yourself out there."

Emma threw her head back in exasperation. She was so tired of having the same conversation over and over with Jennifer. Emma knew that she meant well and was only trying to be helpful, but she couldn't understand why Jennifer refused to accept that she wasn't interested in dating yet.

"We're going to Insurrection tonight," Jennifer continued. "You should come with us. Tonight's the grand opening, everybody will be there."

"Jen, you know I really don't like clubbing."

"You used to. I think you don't like doing anything but sitting at home reading nursing journals and romance novels."

Emma knew Jennifer was right, she needed to be living life and socializing. Since Brock's death, her means of coping with her loss was to focus on college and her nursing degree. She threw herself into work in order to mask the pain and the emptiness that his death had left in her life. That's the way she had survived for the first couple of years after Brock's death. Now it had become as much a habit as a way of coping.

She had little interest in dating because she honestly believed that her one chance at love died with Brock on that snowy mountain slope. Brock was the love of her life; her soul mate. She couldn't imagine how someone else could ever make her feel the love that she felt with him. She was resigned to the belief that she would never find the type of love she had with Brock, so rather than risk finding that to be true, she instead didn't try.

There was a part of her that wanted to go out and live life again, a part that still had hope for a 'happily ever after'. Deep down Emma was tired of going to bed alone, and she was tired of falling asleep to the muffled sounds of Jennifer and Chase making love in the next room. She missed the intimacy and tenderness of another's touch. But that hopeful part that still yearned for love, that part of her didn't know how to begin to live again. Even if she wanted to go out and have fun, she didn't know how to go about it any longer.

"Come on, Em. You deserve to have some fun. Especially after the hard week you've had." Jennifer pressed. "Besides, it's walking distance so you can leave anytime you like and be home in five minutes."

Emma thought about the offer. She really had no plans other than doing laundry and reading medical journals. It would be another dull Saturday night and she didn't really relish the thought of being alone again while everyone her age was out having fun.

"Maybe I will," Emma said. "Yeah, why not? I can go for a little while I guess."

"Oh great! We'll have so much fun!" Jennifer was excited. They hadn't been out together clubbing in literally years.

Chase entered the room, this time fully dressed. He sat at the table next the Jennifer, took her bowl and started eating her cereal.

"Hey, that was mine!" Jennifer protested.

"Was, being the key word," he laughed and took another spoonful. "What's gonna be so much fun?"

"Em's going to the club with us tonight!"

"Really? That's great," Chase agreed. "Jack is meeting us there too. You remember Jack, don't you?"

"Oh, I remember Jack." Emma rolled her eyes. "Sorry to disappoint you Chase, but I just don't think this Jack thing is going to happen for me."

Jack was one of Chase's friends that he had tried to set Emma up with on a date. He was a nice enough guy, but she had no interest in him. Jack was so unlike Brock. Brock was a quiet, thoughtful guy; the strong silent type. Jack was a gregarious frat brother type who was a loud party animal. No, the Jack thing would never happen for her.

Chase laughed. "Don't worry, that ship has sailed. He's dating someone now, and she's coming with."

"That won't be awkward will it?" Jennifer asked.

"Please. Why would it bother me?"

"Being the odd girl out with no date," Jennifer said.

"You are sooo compassionate," Emma scoffed. "If I wanted a date, I could have one."

"Why don't you? What about calling that guy from work? What's his name? The one with the dreamy eyes." Jennifer tilted her head and batted her eyes mockingly.

"David?" Emma blushed. She thought back to the moment in the parking garage when she had kissed him. They had not spoken since the kiss and she was embarrassed to face him. So, no, she was not ready to face David; and she was certainly not bold enough to ask him out on a date, though for a moment she considered how nice it would be to spend time with him.

"That's it. David."

"I barely know him. Besides, let's not go overboard. I said I'd go out for a little while. I want to see the club and listen to the music. That's all. So, let's leave it at that."

"There's going to be lots of singles there," Chase added. "If you want to dance, you'll have plenty of opportunity. Who knows? Maybe you'll meet someone."

The rest of the day, Emma spent cleaning the apartment and doing laundry. In the afternoon she went out for a walk. Her apartment complex was in the downtown area, within walking distance to many shops, restaurants, and just about everything. She loved walking through the city on her days off, window shopping and exploring. Especially now that it was autumn, and the weather was getting cooler again.

She paused at a clothing store and admired the new fall dresses in the window display. One dress in particular caught her eye. It was blue and black with a geometric blocking pattern, sophisticated yet youthful, something she could wear out to dinner and dancing. She admired the outfit for a moment through the window, thinking it would have been something Brock would have liked her to wear.

She continued to walk down the street until she found herself in front of the Insurrection. It was closed until the evening. Posters announcing the big grand opening lined the bottom of the tinted windows. She pressed her hands up against the darkened window pane to peer inside. Through the tinted glass she could make out the interior. There was a large chrome bar that stretched the entire length of one wall with tables throughout the interior. Further back she could she a large dance floor with an array of colored spotlights overhead that would no doubt provide a laser light show while dance music blasted from the massive speakers.

Emma took a step back from the window and thought about days not so long ago that she would go dancing at clubs just like this one. She, Brock, and their friends. That was more than four years ago, but it felt like a lifetime. She had not been out with friends since Brock died; maybe it was time. As she peered through the darkened windows, she suddenly felt nervously excited about going out for the first time in years.

She stepped back and looked at her reflection in the window. Who was the frumpy old maid staring back at her? She barely recognized her reflection, wearing baggy sweatpants and an over-sized sweatshirt. Her hair was pulled back into a ponytail and she had no makeup on.

"Ugh," she groaned as she looked at the reflection. That wasn't her in the window, it was some spinster with half a dozen cats at

home. She turned away from the stranger in
the window and headed back down the street to
the dress shop she had passed earlier.

CHAPTER 6

When Emma and Jennifer arrived at the Insurrection late that evening, the place was already jam-packed with what seemed like all the city's young and beautiful hipsters. The atmosphere was electric with the sound of the dance music pounding from the massive speakers so loudly that the floor vibrated to the beat; even the air seemed to pulse to the rhythm.

They paused just inside the door and stood on their tiptoes, trying to find Chase among the crowd. He promised to meet them there and hold a table.

"Do you see him?" Emma shouted over the blaring music.

"No," Jennifer yelled back. "Let's head over to the bar."

They squeezed through the crowd, looking for Chase along the way. When they finally reached the bar, it was a relief to find the music was not as loud, and Chase seated at a table waiting for them. With him was his friend Jack, a rather good-looking guy with a head full of thick curly brown hair and a slight beard. Emma smiled at seeing him, after all, he was a nice man and the fact he had a date relieved her of any anxiety of seeing him again.

"Hey babe," Chase greeted Jennifer with a kiss that was a little too long for the short amount of time they had been apart. It was evident that he had been there a while and was already drunk.

"Wow, Emma!" Jack stood up and gave her a quick hug. "You look fantastic!"

Emma did look stunning. After seeing her frumpy appearance in the reflection earlier that day, she had gone back to the dress shop and bought the color-block dress she had admired in the window display. It made her feel nice that Jack noticed.

"Hi Jack. How are you?" Emma gave him a slight hug back before they sat down at the table.

"Been good," he smiled. "Just a lot of work lately. Business is good at the moment."

"What is it you do again?" Emma asked only as a courtesy and to make conversation.

"Real Estate," he replied.

It was then that Emma remember exactly the reason she didn't care for Jack. He sold real estate. Not that there was anything wrong with the profession, it was just that Jack had that stereotypical salesman personality; the kind that talked and talked and talked about his job as if he were the housing guru and everyone needed to listen while he educated them on every little aspect of the real estate market.

"Oh, I remember," Emma almost grimaced. She quickly changed the topic before Jack went off on a tirade about some home buyer that couldn't make a decision, or some home inspector that caused a contract to fall through. "Where's your girlfriend?"

"My girlfriend?" He was surprised. "I'm not seeing anybody."

"Oh? Chase said you were dating someone."

"No. I don't know where he got that."

Emma and Jack both turned and glared at Chase.

"Ok, Ok!" Chase admitted with amusement. "I thought you guys could give it one more try. Besides, both of you are single and need at night out; so, what's the big deal?"

Before either Emma or Jack could respond Jennifer grabbed Chase by the arm and pulled him toward the dance floor. "Let's go dance!" Then the couple melted into the crowd leaving Emma and Jack in awkward silence.

"I'm sorry. I had nothing to do with this." Jack looked embarrassed.

"It's all right." It irritated her, but she tried not to show it. It wasn't Jack's fault that they had been set up.

"So, what's the deal?" Jack asked after a few moments

"The deal?"

"What is it about me that offends you so much?" Jack asked defensively. "I mean, do you find me ugly? Is it my breath? What?"

"I'm sorry." Emma suddenly realized how rude she must seem. She had no interest in Jack for a long list of reasons, the main one was his annoying shop talk about real estate but most the other reasons had little to do with him. It wasn't his shortcomings that pushed her away.

"Honestly, Jack. You're a nice guy, and obviously handsome. It's just not the right time for me. I'm not looking to date anyone."

"I see." He was clearly relieved at her response. "You know, Chase told me about your fiancé. I'm sorry for your loss."

"Thank you. But Chase needs to mind his own business."

"I can't imagine how difficult that was for you. Just so you know, we can hang out and chat, even dance if you like, without having to be on a date. You know, I can be a friend without having to take it any further."

Emma finally looked at him instead of past him into the crowd. It wasn't his fault that Chase had tried to play match-maker again. And it certainly wasn't his fault she was still in mourning four years after Brock's passing. Jack was a nice guy so why should she hold any ill feelings toward him about her personal situation?

She managed a smile. "You're right. This doesn't have to be a date. We can have a good time as just friends."

A waitress arrived at the table. "Can I get you a drink?"

"How 'bout a Corona," Jack told the waitress. "What about you Emma?"

"Can I get a Paloma, please?"

"Oooh, that sounds good," Jennifer said as she returned to her seat at the table. "I'll have that too. Tell the bartender not to be stingy with the tequila either."

"Anything else?" The waitress asked. "We have tequila shooters for a dollar tonight."

"Is it the top shelf or some cheap well?" Jennifer asked, referring to the quality and brand of the tequila.

The waitress sighed loudly and put one hand on her hip. "It's a dollar. What do you think?"

"So, it's turpentine," Jack laughed. "We'll take four shots. No, make it five. Bring the lady one shot from the top shelf and one from the well. Let's see if she can tell the difference."

"Oh, I can tell the difference," Jennifer assured him. "But if you want to buy me two shots I'll take 'em."

"Ok. That's two Paloma cocktails. Two coronas. Four tequila shots and a fifth from the top shelf." The waitress repeated back to them. "I'll have it right out for you."

Just as she was leaving to get their drinks the waitress gave Jack a smile and a quick wink. He grinned back sheepishly.

"I saw that," Emma laughed once the waitress was gone. "She was coming on to you."

"She's just working her tips up," Jack laughed.

"Well, hitting on someone else's man is not the way to do it." Jennifer added.

"It's all right," Emma said. "Jack and I have agreed we're here as friends, nothing more. Let her flirt; maybe Jack can get us some free drinks."

"Still, it's rude. And what a bitch! 'It's a dollar, what do you think'," Jennifer mocked. "Only a slut flirts with a guy when it's obvious he's with someone else."

"Oh Jen. You would, and you have." Emma laughed. "Wasn't that how you got Chase?"

"Speaking of, where is Chase?" Jack asked.

"I left him at the bar. He ran into one of his old frat brothers and started reminiscing about the good old days." Jennifer faked a yawn. "I had to leave before they put me to sleep."

"Wonder who it is?" Jack stood up and peered toward the bar like a meerkat. Jack and Chase were longtime friends and had pledged in the same fraternity; so, if Chase had run into an old frat brother, he wanted to know which one. He spotted Chase at the bar, chatting and laughing with a tall handsome blonde. "Well, hell! That's Finn! I've not seen him since my freshman year."

"When the drinks come, start a tab, would ya? I'm wanna go say hello." Jack opened his wallet and dropped a credit card onto the table. Without waiting for a response, he darted through the crowd like someone had shouted 'free beer'.

"Good lord, what is it with frat guys?" Emma said as she watched Jack disappear into the crowd. "I never understood the infatuation fraternity brothers have for each other."

"It's all so homoerotic, isn't it? All those hot boys living together in a house, with their hush-hush rituals, and their secret handshakes." Jennifer laughed dismissively. "You know they all messed around together and passed it off as hazing."

"I wouldn't be surprised."

"After getting a look at that frat brother they both ran after I can understand why. He'd turned the pope gay."

"I thought the pope was gay." Emma laughed.

The waitress arrived with two cocktails and sat them on napkins in front of the women. "Sorry but your dates snatched the shooters and beers from me at the bar," she explained. "Can I bring you a couple more?"

Emma took Jack's credit card from off the table and handed it to the waitress. "Yes, two shots, please. And he'd like to start a tab."

"Do you want the special or will that be the top shelf tequila?" The waitress smirked as she accepted the card.

"Jack's paying," Jennifer pointed out. "Let's get the good stuff."

As Emma watched the waitress walk away her eyes turned toward the end of the bar where Jack and Chase were chatting with their old frat brother. He was standing and leaning on the bar with his back to her but even from behind he seemed very familiar. He was tall with shoulder-length blonde hair, broad shoulders and a strong athletic build. Not many men had a butt like that; round and firm that stuck out enough to accentuate his narrow hips. His jeans hugged his rear and upper thighs tightly, but she noticed that the waist of his pants was crumpled from the cinch of his belt as if he had to wear a size larger in order to fit his butt and legs. She sighed at the sight of him and wondered if he was as handsome from the front as he was from the back. Then he turned slightly, and Emma saw his face.

"Oh my God!" She gasped.

"What is it?" Jennifer asked and immediately looked in the direction Emma was staring. "Is that bitch of a waitress flirting with Chase?"

"Jen, that's Dr. Russo at the bar!"

"Dr. Russo?"

"Yes! Russo. The doctor from work."

As if he sensed her talking about him, Dr. Russo turned and looked toward Emma. Their eyes locked briefly, and Emma sank back into her chair and pulled her hair over her face hoping he did not see her.

"You mean the doctor who's been an a-hole to you?"

"That's the one."

"Where is he?" Jennifer raised out of her seat and scanned the crowd.

"Don't look! Don't look!" Emma grabbed her by the wrist and pulled her back into her seat. "It's the guy with Chase and Jack."

"You're kidding! That hottie is your Dr. Yummy? The dude that is bullying you at work?" She sounded pleased. "Oh wow. I wouldn't mind if he abused me a little bit. Maybe a little spanky."

"Stop it! It's not funny! Please tell me he didn't see me."

"I don't think he recognized you."

"How do you know?" Emma raised her head slightly and peeped through her hair.

"The guys are coming back and he's still at the bar by himself."

"Thank God!" The last thing she wanted was to be confronted by Dr. Russo on her night off. "I just can't deal with him tonight. I came out to forget about work."

Emma stood up and gathered her purse. She was ready to leave. She had agreed to go out to the club in order to relax and forget about the horrible week she had, but instead, she found herself at the same bar as the man she was trying to get away from.

"What are you doing?" Jennifer asked.

"I need to leave. I thought I could do this but I'm just too tired tonight," she answered. "Had I known he would be here I'd have never agreed to come out."

"What's going on?" Chase asked as he arrived back at the table. "You're not leaving, are you? You just got here."

Jennifer was frustrated. She had tried to convince Emma for months to step out and when she finally did, she was ready to leave within only minutes of arriving. It was as if Emma was looking for any excuse to go.

"Your friend over there has her all flustered," Jennifer answered.

"You mean Finn?" Chase asked. "Yeah, he had that effect on all the girls in college, and honestly, he had some brothers pretty rattled too. Do you want me to introduce you?"

"No! That won't be necessary." Emma snapped.

"That's Dr. Yummy from the hospital." Jennifer laughed.

"Oh! That's Dr. Yummy?" Chase opened his eyes wide and grinned. Finn Russo was a hero in his fraternity, and he could see why Emma would have called him Dr. Yummy. What surprised him was that everybody liked Finn; that is, apparently everybody except Emma.

"Jen! You told him about that?" Emma put her hands on her hips and glared at Jennifer. "How could you?"

"I didn't know it was a big secret," Jennifer said. "And what are the chances that Dr. Yummy would turn out to Chase's frat brother."

Chase, Jennifer and Jack all began to laugh.

"It's not funny!" Emma protested.

"Sorry Emma, but actually it is," Jack said.

"You knew about this too?" Emma gave Jennifer a sour glare. "What'd you do, post it on Instagram or take out a Facebook ad?"

"No!" Jennifer said. "And I didn't tell him anything."

"It's my fault," Chase admitted though his continued laughing revealed no sign of regret. "It was a funny story and I may have mentioned it to Jack."

"I hate you all," Emma looked as if she were about to cry.

"Oh, boo hoo, Em! Get over it," Jennifer said. "You're not the first person to make an ass of yourself in front of a guy."

"Well, I'm going home. You guys can stay here and laugh at my expense, but I don't have to sit and be the victim." Emma slung her purse over her shoulder and prepared to storm off. "You all have a good time."

"Oh Em, don't go away mad. We're just teasing." Jack took her by the arm gently. "Stay and have a few drinks."

Emma paused. This was her first time out without Brock, and part of her felt as if she was betraying his memory by even being there. She wanted to go home, not just because of the teasing, but because she felt uncomfortable. Even with friends and in a huge crowd, she felt alone without Brock.

"Let me get my jacket and I'll walk you home," Jack offered.

"No, please! You stay. I'll be fine." Emma didn't wait for approval. She turned and started through the crowd toward the exit.

The club had gotten a lot busier since she had arrived, and she had to squeeze herself through all the people. She saw an opening in the crowd, so Emma made a quick lunge to get through. When she did, she bumped into someone and the drink he was holding flew up and splattered all over his shirt and the leather jacket draped over his arm.

"Oh, I'm so sorry," she shouted over the noise. When she saw the man's face, she grimaced and silently cursed her bad luck. Of all the people she could have bumped into, it was Dr. Russo who stood there soaked in liquor.

Dr Russo brushed at his shirt and then the dripping leather jacket. "Don't worry about it," he said. "It was cheap bourbon. The jacket on the other hand …"

Russo's eyes widen when he realized it was Emma, and he gave a heavy sigh as if she should have known. "My favorite nurse," he said in a tone that made it clear she was anything but that.

"I'm so so sorry," she apologized again. "I was trying to get to the exit and didn't see you."

"Don't sweat it. The jacket was ready for the cleaner anyway." He opened his arms and looked at his shirt, soaked through to his skin. "As for the shirt, it'll all come out in the wash."

"I'll be happy to pay for the cleaners."

"That's not necessary. Isn't bourbon a good leather cleaner, anyway?" He replied and again brushed at the coat.

"Is it?"

"No, not really. I'm just trying to be nice." He answered, this time a little light-heartedly.

"Oh. I'm so sorry. Let me take it and have it cleaned at least."

"It's fine."

"Please, I insist."

"I said, don't worry about it." He answered firmly. He was becoming short with her persistence.

"Okay, if you're sure," she relented.

"I'm sure."

"Well, you have a good night." Emma moved past him and continued to make her was to the exit.

"Hey, wait!" He shouted and headed after her. "Is that it?"

She paused and turned back to him. "What do you mean?"

"You can't spare a minute to say hello? I guess you're wanting to get back to your date."

"I'm here with friends, not a date. Besides, I suspect I'm the last person in this place you'd want to chat with."

"Well, not the very last." He smiled sheepishly. "I think Eric Trump is around here somewhere."

Emma giggled lightly. Was this a joke he was playing on her or was Dr. Russo seriously being nice? She didn't know what to say and stood there looking at him dumbfounded.

"So where, if not back to your boyfriend, are you headed so fast?"

"I said he's not my boyfriend. I was trying to leave."

"Leave?" He looked at his watch. "It's not even midnight. It's still early."

"Maybe for you, but I'm just not into a crowd tonight."

"Sorry?" He shouted over the pounding beat and leaned down with his ear toward her. "Apparently, the DJ just pumped up the volume a few decibels."

"I said, I'm not into crowds," she shouted back.

He shook his head and pointed to his ear indicating he couldn't hear her. At that point, he took her by the hand and led her through the crowd until they were at the club entrance where the music was no longer so overpowering.

"Sorry, the music was just too loud to have a conversation," he explained as he guided her toward a corner where they could speak. "Is this better?"

"Yes, much." Emma agreed. "What I was trying to say I was leaving. I'm not in the mood for all this noise and bumper to bumper crowds."

"I hear that. I'm feeling a little claustrophobic myself. I prefer having a drink in a more intimate setting, maybe with some light jazz playing in the background. I don't care for this pounding racket with some guy screaming lyrics that make no sense."

Emma laughed.

"What's so funny? You actually like this kind of music?" He laughed lightly with her.

"Well, I do like to dance." She answered with an off-handed shrug.

"To that?" He laughed. "I like to dance too, but I'd rather do it to a good old-fashioned Tango or Samba rather than that crazy grand mal seizure type dancing."

"Tango? Samba? I don't believe you." She lightly touched his hand but immediately withdrew when she realized she was giggling and acting like a schoolgirl.

"Yes, I can do the tango." He flashed a smile and stepped toward her assuming a more casual and intimate closeness. He lowered his voice as if he were betraying a secret. "I didn't say I was good at it though."

"So, if you don't like crowds, and hate loud music, what are you doing here?" Emma inquired.

"Let's just call it a lapse in judgment. This really isn't my usual type of stomping grounds. The club manager is an old friend, and he insisted I show up and wish him well."

"I see."

"Since I've done my duty," he looked down at the linen shirt that was clinging to his chest, "and I'm a little wet. I suppose I'll be heading out myself. Could I offer you a lift?"

"I'll walk. I don't live that far away."

"Nonsense! I can't let you walk home alone this time of night."

"Seriously, I don't live that far away. I'll be fine."

"Then at least let me accompany you. You shouldn't be walking the streets alone at night."

Emma felt the impulse to continue to resist, but she really did want to continue the conversation. This was a different side of Dr. Russo, and it fascinated her. She wanted to know more.

"All right, if you're leaving anyway, I don't see the harm."

"Very good," he said and gently placed his hand on her back to guide her out the door onto the sidewalk. "Oh. Did you bring a rap?"

"A rap?"

"Yes. There's a chill in the air tonight."

"Oh, you mean a jacket. No, it didn't seem that cool when I came out."

"Here, take mine." He placed his leather jacket around her shoulders without giving her time to resist.

Emma wanted to decline out of politeness, especially since he was wearing a wet shirt from the drink she had spilled; surely, he was a little cold himself. But when he placed the coat around her, the aroma of it was intoxicating; not just the smell of the bourbon, but the scent of fine leather mingled with the subtle musky smell of him, and the distinct scent of his cologne. She inhaled deeply and pulled the jacket tightly around her as if she were wrapping herself in an embrace.

"Better?"

"Oh yes, thank you. But now you're cold."

"I'm not cold. I grew up in Norway, this is like a summer heat wave for me."

"Norway? I would never have thought! I knew I could hear a slight accent, but I never would have guessed Norway."

"My parents sent me to English schools and most of my friends were American. Plus, when I was a teenager, I wanted to be a weatherman on the tele, so I worked diligently on eliminating my accent. We moved to America when I was 16 so my accent is rather subtle now."

"Well, it's nice. I like the way you are so precise with every word," she smiled then quickly turned away and blushed. She realized she was flirting but she couldn't help herself. "Do you speak Norwegian?"

"I'm a bit rusty. I haven't used it in years."

"Say something." Emma asked in an almost schoolgirl giddiness. "I love the sound of foreign languages."

He laughed. "Du ser nydelig ut i måneskinnet." When he spoke, it was with a strong accent but at the same time his words were gentle and warm as if he were lulling a child to sleep.

"That's beautiful, it sounds like German."

"Well, it is a Germanic language, so they sound very similar if you don't know the language."

"What does it mean; what you said a moment ago?" She clutched at his arm like an excited schoolgirl.

"I said, you look beautiful in the moonlight."

"Oh." She blushed again and then there was a moment of silence as Emma didn't know how to respond. She struggled for what to say next, then suddenly she blurted out, "So, a weatherman?"

"What can I say? Honestly, I still haven't decided what I want to be when I grow up." He grinned and gave her a wink.

"I can see you as a TV weatherman. You've got that look, more so than that of a doctor."

"Oh really, how so?"

"Tall, handsome, blonde. Like you should be on the cover of a romance novel rather than in hospital scrubs."

"That's been my problem. People have always looked at me like I'm some bubble-headed blonde jock. I had to fight that stigma all through college and medical school."

"Oh, poor you," Emma laughed. "It must have been so hard being physically perfect."

"Perfect? Ha! I'm far from perfect. It's all smoke and mirrors. When you get down to it, I'm just a whole lot of ugly parts put together to make one hell of a good-looking man." He laughed loudly. "Here, look!" He turned so they were standing face to face, then pointed at his nose.

Emma looked hard at his face. She squinted her eyes and studied his nose. After a moment, she shrugged. "What am I looking for?"

"You don't see it?"

"Not really. You could use a trim up in there, other than that I see a perfectly normal nose."

"Look again." He tilted his head back further and point at the tip of his nose.

"See? My nares. One is larger than the other."

Emma leaned in and looked closer. "You're not serious; they look exactly the same."

"You're not looking close enough." He wrapped his arm around her, and they continued walking. "I have a lot of flaws and errors. You're just seeing the whole picture and not the individual parts."

"Exactly! When you look at a painting, do you see the painting or just the brush strokes? If you're that self-critical, I can only imagine how I must look to you."

"Absolutely beautiful."

"Huh?"

"You look absolutely beautiful tonight." He repeated.

Her cheeks turned pink, and she turned shyly away. She didn't know how to respond to the compliment and wondered if he was serious or playing a cruel trick.

"What about you? Did you always want to be a nurse?"

"I'm not going to say. You'll laugh."

"You laughed at me. You owe me one."

He pulled her close as they continued to walk down the street. Emma was about to tell him they were going the wrong direction, that she lived two blocks the other way, but she stopped herself. He was captivating, and she wanted to prolong the walk. It seemed like a dream and at any moment she expected to wake up; so, taking the long route home suddenly seemed appealing.

"Go on. What do you want to be when you grow up?" He asked.

"You promise not to laugh?"

"Of course not! I will promise no such thing. I hope it's something hysterical that I can tease you about for the rest of my life."

She punched him in the side playfully. "You're terrible!"

"Okay, I'll try not to laugh, but no promises."

"Well, when I was a little girl, I wanted to be an acrobat and perform with Cirque de Sole." She paused just waiting for him to laugh. She hadn't shared that dream with anyone before, not even Brock; she wondered why she suddenly revealed her secret to him so easily.

He stopped walking and turned to look at her with a raised eyebrow. "Seriously," he asked with a glimmer in his green eyes. "Are you serious, or is that some pickup line you use on guys you meet at bars?"

"For your information, I don't pick up guys at bars," she scoffed at his implication. "I have never!"

"Sorry, I didn't mean to suggest you were… you know."

They continued walking in silence.

Emma didn't want to create tension and felt badly that she may have spoiled the moment by responding harshly to him. She decided to lighten the mood again.

"As to the original question," she said. "Yes, I'm totally serious. I wanted to be in Cirque du Soleil when I was a little girl. My dad took me to a performance when I was around nine and they mesmerized me. I couldn't think of anything else for months afterward."

"Really? Wow!" Russo put his arm back around her. "I can see you doing something like that. You have that petite gymnast build. Why didn't you pursue it?"

"We used to have a tall tree in my backyard. One day I decided to tie a rope to one of the highest branches so I could swing from it and practice. Unfortunately, I got halfway up the tree and realized I was afraid of heights."

Finn chuckled. "That could be detrimental to a career on the high wire."

"I literally was so petrified that I couldn't move. I was frozen there, 15 feet off the ground, clinging to a tree limb for dear life." Emma began to laugh hysterically. "My mom had to call the fire department to come and get me down."

"How awful." Finn said, but his expression revealed he was fighting back his laughter.

She again punched him in his side.

"Ouch! What was that for? I didn't laugh!"

"No, but you're wanting too."

They continued strolling down the street chatting and laughing with his arm wrapped snuggly around her. Anyone who knew them would have been stunned to see them together, but not as much as Emma was herself at the situation. She thought Dr. Russo hated her, at least he acted like he did at work. He was continually snapping and yelling at her, correcting her constantly and rarely did he offer any words of encouragement. Frankly, up to that moment she thought he was one of the most despicable men she had ever encountered. Sure, he was pleasant to the eye, but he was also at times mean and abrupt. But at that moment, in the cool moonlit night, all that animosity seemed so far away, replaced by a genuine, though surprising, fondness between them.

As they walked, Emma had given him directions taking one corner after another until they were back the front of the Insurrection night club again. At first Finn was so engaged in their conversation he barely noticed. Then, he looked around and realized where they were.

"Are we going in circles?" Finn asked.

"Sort of. I live just two blocks down this street."

"Why didn't we go that way in the first place?"

She smiled. "You seemed so sure of where you wanted to go, I hated to tell you we were going the wrong direction."

He laughed. "Well, I'm glad. I've enjoyed the walk."

They continued the short distance until they arrived at Emma's apartment complex.

"This is it," she announced. "Home sweet home."

Finn looked up at the building. It was one of the older buildings in the downtown area and had the art déco style architecture that he admired. He had passed it many times on the way to work and often stopped to marvel at its stately beauty.

"I've always loved this building. Looks like you can walk to a lot of good restaurants."

"Yeah, and I don't have to drive other than to work."

"Cool. I've always wondered what it looked like on the inside." Finn offered a not so subtle hint.

They stood there somewhat awkwardly. Emma wasn't sure what was supposed to happen next, and apparently neither did Finn. They hadn't been on a date, so a good-night kiss didn't seem appropriate. But she wanted to be kissed by him.

"Well, thank you for walking me home," Emma finally said. "It was a nice way to end the evening."

"It doesn't have to end yet, does it?" Finn stepped close to her and looked in her eyes hopefully. "You could invite me up?"

Emma was stunned. This had to be a dream and any moment she'd wake up. Who was this man that was so enticing and what had he done with the nasty Dr. Russo? She gazed into his eyes. At that moment, she wanted to throw caution to the wind and invite him to her apartment. She longed for him to take her into his arms and kiss her passionately. But instead, she took a step back and composed herself. She wasn't sure what had happened to Dr. Russo, whether he had drunk too much or if he was playing some sort of game with her. Regardless she was not about to risk making herself vulnerable to being hurt. Then her thoughts turned to Brock, and she felt guilty that she would even consider allowing another man, especially this one, to take his place even for a moment.

"Did I say something wrong?" Finn saw her expression harden as she stepped away from him.

"No, I don't think it's a good idea."

"Oh, you mean because of work."

"Not just that. I mean I'm not that kind of girl." She said honestly. She had never had a one-night stand. Brock was her one and only boyfriend and they had dated exclusively. She had never been with anyone else before or since Brock.

"It's not like I'm some stranger you picked up at a bar." He said defensively. He didn't want her to think that he was accustomed to going home with just anyone any more than she was.

"Well, actually that's exactly what you are," Emma replied. "I've only known you a week, and honestly, until tonight I didn't even like you."

Finn laughed lightly. "So, are you saying you like me now?"

Emma blushed. "I'm saying I don't know you that way. And besides, walking me home doesn't entitle you to anything more than a 'thank-you' and 'good-night'."

"I see," he said playfully. "But surely, lending you my jacket entitles me to something. And the fact that I'm walking around with a bourbon-soaked shirt freezing my nipples off should count for something too. Don't you think?"

"Should I apologize again?"

"Come here, you." He grabbed her by the arm and pulled her too him.

She looked at him with anticipation. Finn tenderly put one arm around her waist and held her tightly against him. With his other hand her gently caressed her cheek then ran his fingers through her hair and cupped the back of Emma's neck. Then he leaned down and brought his mouth close to hers and hesitated briefly. She felt the warmth of his breath against her lips and she closed her eyes in sweet anticipation. Then his lips touched hers, lightly at first but then more urgently with passion.

Emma melted against him; her body helpless to resist him. Her legs felt weak and wobbly as she surrendered to his embrace, and for the first time she understood what the word swoon meant. She had never felt so overcome by a kiss. Not even her great love Brock had that much power over her with a single kiss.

After a moment, Finn released her and took a step back. He looked at Emma with satisfaction like a conquering hero waiting for the roar from an adoring crowd. Satisfied, that Emma was completely spellbound by his kiss he happily bounced back down the steps to the sidewalk leaving her speechless.

"Hey, I'll pick you up for dinner tomorrow at seven." He called back as he walked away. "Be waiting here out front."

Emma paused and looked back at him and answered playfully, "What makes you think I'd go out to dinner with you?"

"Because you like me, don't bother trying to deny it."

"No, I don't! Not even a little," she giggled. "Besides, I have plans for dinner already."

"Cancel them. You know you want to." He said confidently and began to head back down the street without waiting for her response.

"I will not," she called after him. She could almost have convinced herself she meant it. Who was he to think she would cancel her plans at the last minute to go out with him? The nerve!

"Of course, you will." Finn raised his hand and waved as he continued walking away. "See you at seven."

Emma watched him swagger away. He was so cocky and confident in his walk, so sure she would drop everything for a chance to have dinner with the great Dr. Russo. She didn't have any plans for dinner, but she held firm that if she did, she wouldn't have cancelled for him.

She pulled the jacket tightly around her and smelled the collar. The scent of him still mingled with the leather. Maybe she would go out with him after all. Maybe.

CHAPTER 7

Emma sat with her legs crossed on the sofa quietly thumbing through a fashion magazine; paying no attention to the content and definitely not reading it. She was killing time; waiting. She glanced at her watch then at the leather jacket draped over the back of a chair. She had planned to take it to the cleaners early that morning, but since it was Sunday, the likelihood of finding a dry cleaner that was open was next to zero. That was just as well, as far as Emma was concerned, since the jacket still held the scent of Finn.

Jennifer and Chase were hugged tightly together on the sofa watching a horror flick. Chase gave Jennifer a slight nudge when he saw Emma impatiently checking her watch again.

"Good article?" Chase asked.

Emma shrugged.

"You know, you could call him," Jennifer said.

"Huh? Call who?" Emma replied.

"Dr. Yummy." Chase blurted out and both he and Jennifer laughed loudly.

"I don't know what you're talking about," Emma flipped the page of her magazine loudly. "And please stop calling him that."

"Come on, Em," Jennifer snickered. "You're clearly waiting on something or somebody. You've looked out the window a dozen times in the past 5 minutes. You're not even looking at the magazine and isn't that the same jacket your Doctor friend was wearing last night at the club?"

"Are you guys hooking up tonight?" Chase lit up at the prospect. "Is that what this is all about?"

"No! We are not hooking up!" Emma snapped. "He just happened to mention he might drop by. You know, to pick up his jacket."

"That'll be great!" Chase sat up. "I was hoping to catch up with him."

"Cool it Chase," Jennifer said. "He's coming to see Em, not you."

"I know, but it's still exciting that she might be dating my old frat brother. We could all hang out and go on double dates. It'll be great." Chase replied.

"We are not dating," Emma pointed out. "We work together and that's as far as it goes."

Emma refused to admit that she had any interest in Dr. Russo; she wouldn't admit it to Chase or Jennifer, not even to herself. Sure, he was handsome, well-bred, stable, and a doctor; and he smelled nice. But she rejected the thought that she felt something for Finn, she simply had no desire to date anyone right now. It was flattering that he had expressed an interest in her, but there was still the issue of the way he treated her at work, and she still felt obligated to remain faithful to Brock.

"Then why is he coming over?" Jenn probed. "And don't say to give him back his coat because you could do that at work tomorrow."

"If you must know, he asked me out for dinner."

"Oh, do tell!" Jennifer replied.

"Well, I'm not going."

"Why the hell not?" Chase was indignant. How could she play hard to get with Finn Russo of all people? He was a demigod back during their frat days, every girl wanted to date him, and every guy wanted to be him. Now, Finn was a doctor and even more of a catch than back in college.

"You've got to be trippin," Chase continued. "You know how many people would love to be in your shoes?"

"Don't be so gay, Chase. Maybe you should date him then." Jennifer teased.

Chase laughed. "If I wanted to switch team, he'd be the one I'd play for and I'm not ashamed to admit that. What's wrong with you, Em?"

"How much time do you have, cause there's a lot of reasons." Emma answered.

"How about just the top two? Because aside from Chase's obvious man-crush, I don't get it either." Jennifer said. "He's to die for! And, he's a freaking doctor!"

"He's also an arrogant bully!" Emma snapped. "He's tormented me at work and treated me like I'm an idiot. Then last night when we were walking, he practically ordered me to be ready for dinner at seven. He didn't ask, he presumed I'd be so taken by him I couldn't say no. I would not go out with him if he were the last man on earth."

Emma tossed her magazine on the coffee table, then got up and walked to the window to peer out at the street.

"Yet there you are, looking out the window for your beau." Jenn giggled.

"I'm only watching so I can give him his coat back." She said as she looked down at the street. Despite her resistance and denials, when Emma saw Dr. Russo walking up the street toward her building, she let out a little sigh. He was dreamy, she thought.

Jennifer noticed the change in Emma's demeanor and the little smile she fought to restrain. "He's out there isn't he." Jennifer jumped up from the couch and joined her in looking out the window. Chase hurried excitedly behind and all three peered out.

On the street below, Finn stopped in front of the building and waited. He checked his watch then looked up and down the street expectantly. He faced the building entrance and checked his watch again.

"What's he waiting on?" Chase questioned. "Why isn't he coming up?"

"Does he know where you live?" Jennifer asked.

"He's waiting because he ordered me to meet him in front of the building at 7 o'clock. He didn't ask, just told me to be there waiting for him."

"That was kinda rude." Jennifer agreed.

The two girls continued to peer out the window while Chase stepped away.

"So, what are you going to do?" Jennifer asked. "You can't just let him stand there waiting."

"Oh yes I can."

The two girls giggled and continued to peek out the window at Finn. Down below, Finn pulled his cell phone out of his pocket apparently answering a call.

"Hey dude!" Chase said loudly behind them.

The girls turned to see Chase on his cell phone. Emma glanced back out the window at Finn on his own cell phone and she immediately knew what was happening. Chase was calling Finn.

"Hang up!" Emma mouthed urgently and tried to grab the phone from him.

Chase turned and blocked her and continued speaking into the phone. "Dude come on up to the apartment. Em's still getting ready so we can have a beer while you wait."

"No. No. No." Emma mouthed and urgently waved her hands.

"Sure! We're in 6b. Just take a left when you get out of the elevator." Chase said then hung up the phone.

Emma put her hands on her hips and scowled at him. "Why did you do that?"

"Because he's a grown man and you're supposed to be a grown woman. If you don't want to go out with the guy, then be a big girl and tell him. Hiding up here and peeking out the window like a cat isn't going to cut it."

"You know, he's right," Jennifer added. "If you don't want to go out just say so. You still have to work with this guy so you can't keep hiding."

"Fine! Just remember this when you need something from me!" Emma scowled.

In a few moments there was a knock at the door and Emma begrudgingly opened it.

"Hey," Finn smiled. "Are you ready to go?"

"Not exactly." She answered uncomfortably and with hesitation. She hated to be in the position to reject him, at least face to face. It would have been much easier had she just hid until he gave up and went away on his own. Now she had to face the man and decline going out with him in person.

"Hey, man!" Chase called out to him. "Come on in! We can have a beer while Em gets ready."

"Oh, great!" Finn replied and happily walked past Emma to where Chase stood. The two men exchanged a quick side hug.

"Grab us a couple beers, will you babe?" Chase instructed Jennifer as if he were placing an order with a waitress.

Jennifer glared at him. "Would you like some chips with that? Maybe some salsa or dip?"

"No hon, just the beers." Chase was oblivious to her scowl and sarcasm.

Jennifer crossed her arms and clinched her teeth, but he was no longer paying attention to her. Reluctantly, she headed to the kitchen to retrieve the beers. As she passed Emma still standing by the front door staring at the two men in dismay, she paused briefly and said under her breath, "Can you believe this? Male bonding at its finest."

"Uh huh," Emma mumbled back. She studied Finn as the two men sat on opposite ends of the sofa and turned their bodies to face each other and began chatting something about football and who would make it to the Superbowl. Jennifer returned with two bottles of beer and presented them to the guys, then gave an exaggerated curtsy. Chase didn't even acknowledge her but continued talking about how they should try to get tickets to the game this year, and that Chase knew a guy who knew another guy that could get tickets.

Jennifer stood next to Emma who had not moved from her spot since opening the door to Finn. The two girls watched in awe as the men reminisced about the good old college days.

"I bet they hooked up in college," Jennifer whispered to Emma.

"You think?" Emma giggled. "They do seem awfully into each other to just be frat bros."

"I bet they've messed around and then acted like they were too drunk to remember it."

"You're crazy, Jen." Emma thought it was funny that Jennifer suspected them of having been intimate in college, but she didn't believe it for a minute.

"Just saying, I've always been suspicious of these frat brothers and the way they fawn over each other. You watch. Any minute they'll start wrestling and pulling at each other's clothes."

Emma laughed out loud, then covered her mouth. The two men glanced over at her for only a moment before resuming their own conversation about how many yards rushing somebody had.

Emma studied Finn closely as he continued to chat excitedly with Chase. He seemed so different to her away from the hospital. He was very animated when he talked displaying almost a boyish excitement; and, he laughed easily and was full of life. At work Finn was just the opposite. He was very deadpan and had a persistent matter-of-fact attitude, although at times he would let his sense of humor shine through if only for a moment. Finn's whole transformation was baffling to her.

Occasionally Finn would look over at Emma and would smile brightly and a wink, then turn back to chatting. Suddenly it occurred to Emma that maybe it wouldn't be such a bad thing for her to go out on a date with this handsome doctor. What was the problem with that? They worked together, but still he wasn't her boss so there was no issue with violating hospital policy.   He was extremely attractive; maybe a little too handsome for her taste.

On the other hand, she found him arrogant and condescending, though those were qualities he shared with most the other men she had dated thus far. Still that wasn't such a put off, she preferred a confident, take-charge type of guy. So why did she object to him?

She continued to question her feelings, oscillating back and forth between how great he was versus how much of a jerk he was at work. She wanted to go out with him, then she didn't; and back and forth the battle raged in her head and her heart. Finally, her head won. Despite his good looks and his charm, Finn had insulted her, bullied her, and belittled her nursing skills. No matter how handsome the good doctor was, and how nice he was presently behaving, he was still a prick in her eyes.

Emma took a long deep breath and settle on the decision that she would not get involved with Dr. Russo. She stood straight up and mentally prepared for the uncomfortable task of sending him on his way. She stepped toward the sofa where the guys were still chatting and cleared her throat loudly to get Finn's attention.

"Ah, sorry," Finn apologized. "I guess we got a little carried away reminiscing. You ready to go?"

"I think we need to talk," she said then turned to glare at Chase. "Privately."

Jennifer walked over and pulled Chase up from the sofa by his arm. "She said privately."

"Okay, I guess I'm being thrown out," Chase whined. "Catch ya later, man!"

"Later!" Finn replied.

Jennifer and Chase retreated down the hallway and disappeared behind their bedroom door. Once Emma was sure they were out of ear shot, she turned to face Finn and nervously began to ring her hands.

"This doesn't seem ominous at all," Finn noted.

"Dr. Russo…" she began as she sat down across from him.

"Finn." He corrected with a nervous laugh. He could sense that what was about to follow would not be good news.

"I'd rather not." Emma said dryly.

"Oh?" He looked down at the floor like a scolded child.

"I don't think this is a good idea."

"Why not?" He asked and continued to hang his head. "Aren't you attracted to me?"

Emma couldn't help but laugh at the question. It was ridiculous to think that any woman wouldn't find him attractive. "Of course, I am. Physically, you're amazing."

"Physically?"

"It's just our work situation."

"Don't worry about work. Lots of doctors and nurses date and nobody cares."

"That's not exactly it." Emma had hoped she could simply say she didn't want to go out and that would be the end of it. She didn't expect that she would have to justify the rejection.

"So, what is the reason? Is it that paramedic guy, David?

"No, it's not David. He's just a friend."

"Then what is it?" Finn looked at the floor and shuffled a foot back and forth.

"Uh… I'm not sure how to say this."

"Spit it out, I'm a grown man so I can take rejection." He glared at her and clinched his jaw. Her stalling was irritating. "The least you can do is to be honest."

"Well, if you want honesty. The truth is… it's you." She didn't intend to be so harsh with him, she wanted to let him down gently. But she was so uncomfortable turning him down that she became angry that he didn't just accept her answer and walk away. Instead, he expected her to give him a reason. So, she decided to go ahead and vent her frustration directly at him.

"You've been a dick to me from day one. You've been mean, rude, condescending; and you've made my job miserable. Then last night, out of the blue, you're suddenly interested in me. I don't get it. You're like Dr. Jekyll and Mr. Hyde. You've been horrible at work and now you're being all James Bond sexy. You're like two different people."

"You think I'm James Bond sexy?" He forced a grin and attempted to ease the tension with humor. However, he didn't think what she said was humorous, in fact, her words were painful to him. He was hurt and uncomfortable, so he attempted to lighten the mood.

"That's all you heard?" She was flustered and red faced. "You know, you're really a jerk!"

"Are you finished?"

"I suppose I am."

Finn stared past her with an unfocused gaze. He bit his lip as he pondered what she had said. For a moment it seemed he was about to cry. Her words stung him deeply. "Sorry you feel that way," he said and walked toward the door. As he was about to leave, he turned back.

"I try to keep my work and my personal lives separate. At the hospital we deal with life and death situations. It's not like we're mindlessly folding sweaters in the mall. What we do, and don't do, affects people's lives. They come into our E.R. for help, and they trust us with their lives. I don't take that responsibility lightly. That's why I don't tolerate incompetence, carelessness, or horseplay. If that makes me a jerk, as you put it, then I'm good with that. In the end it makes me a better doctor and a decent human being. I'd much rather be a jerk, than face myself in the mirror after I screwed up and hurt someone. Sorry if you don't get that."

"There's a big difference between being professional and being a jerk. I worked hard to get my nursing license and I'm good at my job! I take my job as seriously as you do."

"Come on, Emma! The first thing you said to me was to call me Dr. Goodbody or Dr. YumYum or whatever silly remark it was," Finn argued back.

"Kenise told me that was your name." Her face turned beet red. "How was I supposed to know she was joking?"

"I don't know, common sense, maybe? Or try reading my name tag. And let's not forget you almost killed a patient, not once but twice!"

Emma closed her eyes tightly and took a deep breath, then exhaled heavily. She was so frustrated she could scream, but instead, she calmed her voice and took a deep cleansing breath. "I think it's time for you to leave."

They stared at each other in silence. Neither wanted their encounter to end in such anger, but it was too late. The situation had escalated too fast to leave on good terms. Finn continued to look at her in disbelief, struggling for something to say.

"I'm sorry," she finally said. "I shouldn't have been so mean to you. You're a good doctor, and I'm sure you're a great guy, but I don't think this thing is going to work out."

"This thing? You mean these feelings we have for each other?"

"Yes. Whatever is happening here, between us. If this goes any further, I'm afraid one of us will get hurt."

"One of us already has." Finn opened the door and stepped into the hallway. He paused a moment, hoping that Emma would ask him to stay, but the invitation did not come. He sighed heavily then closed the door behind him leaving her in her bitter silence.

Emma crossed her arms, then rubbed one hand on her forehead as she tried not to cry. She was disappointed, not with Dr. Russo but with herself. She knew in her heart he was a good man. She enjoyed the time they had spent walking together and how easily their conversation had flowed. He checked all her boxes: he was stable, mature, gainfully employed, had a great sense of humor, and was very sexy. Any woman would have been happy to be asked out on a date by Finn Russo. But instead of opening herself to the possibility of a relationship, she sabotaged it before it even started.

Despite all her excuses, Emma knew the truth behind why she was so reluctant to go out with Russo. It wasn't because he had been rude to her at work. It was because of Brock. She couldn't bring herself to let go of his memory. For her to be with someone else she had to let Brock go; and, she wasn't ready to do that. She compared every man to Brock, and every one of them came up short in her eyes. In truth, Brock was far from perfect in life, but her memory told a different story. In her grief she remembered Brock as being bigger, stronger and more perfect than he had been in real life. He also had one more unimpeachable quality that no other man possessed, in death Brock didn't make mistakes.

CHAPTER 8

Emma headed to the equipment room for supplies to restock the patient rooms. As she stepped inside, Kenise pushed in behind her and closed the door.

"Okay, girl." Kenise placed her hand on her hip and stared at her in anticipation. "What gives?"

"What do you mean?" Emma had no idea what she was talking about.

"There's so much tension in the air this morning you could cut it with a knife."

"I haven't noticed."

"Oh, please!" Kenise tapped her foot. "You and Dr. Russo are avoiding each other like the plague this morning. And, you and that paramedic are cutting eyes at each other like you were caught passing love notes in elementary school. So, spill the beans."

Emma closed her eyes and sighed heavily. She was avoiding Finn, which was easy since he wasn't even acknowledging her presence. He wasn't angry at her, that much she could tell because when they passed in the hallway, he glanced at her with a sad expression that was a mix of embarrassment and regret. So, they were mutually avoiding each other out of discomfort rather than out of anger or resentment.

Then there was the situation with David. This was the first day they had worked together since she had abruptly kissed him. She didn't know what to say to him, all she could do was look at him and a blush. She didn't know how he felt about it. Did he enjoy the kiss or was he as embarrassed about it as she was? She didn't know what to do, so rather than directly speak to him she opted to run in the opposite direction whenever she saw him approaching.

Kenise leaned back against the closed door, determined that Emma was not leaving until she came clean with what was going on. "You're not going anywhere until you spill your guts."

"It's nothing."

"If it's nothing then why so evasive?"

"Kenise, it's not a big deal." Emma continued to resist.

"At least you now admit there's something going on. Come on, it can't be all that bad, can it?"

Just then the door pushed open against Kenise's back.

"Just a moment," Kenise called out and continued to block the door from opening completely.

"Kenise, it's me. Open up!" Pam whispered through to the slight opening in the doorway.

Kenise stepped away and Pam quickly slipped inside and closed the door back.

"So, what's going on?" Pam's eyes widen in excitement, fully expecting to hear some earth-shattering gossip. "Was I right? Did I win?"

"Hush up a minute, I'm trying to find out." Kenise insisted.

"What do you mean, 'did I win'?" Emma asked.

"Never mind that," Kenise dismissed. "So, tell me what's going on with you."

"There's nothing going on, I told you." Emma was frustrated with the inquisition.

"Fine! Be that way if you like, but just remember this in the future when you need someone to help you out."

"How is my telling you my personal business helping you?"

"Because she's got $10 riding on you." Pam chuckled. "And I've got $5. So, spill the beans girlfriend."

"You're gambling on me and my personal life?"

"Honey, you're part of our nursing family now, you don't have a personal life." Kenise laughed. "Especially if you bring it to work."

Emma crossed her arms and looked up at the ceiling, then looked back at them and bit her lip. "I didn't realize it was so obvious."

"Well, it is. You and Dr. Russo and David scatter like cockroaches whenever you see each other coming." Kenise replied. "It's pretty obvious something's up."

"It's okay," Pam relented. "Obviously you don't want to talk about it, so we'll leave you alone."

"Speak for yourself, girl!" Kenise cocked her head back. "Nobody's leaving this room until I get some answers."

Emma shook her head in defeat. "Okay, I'll tell you, but you can't breathe a word to anyone else. Promise?"

"Cross my heart," Pam agreed. "I won't say a word."

The both looked at Kenise and waited. She was oddly silent seeming to be mulling over Emma's request.

"I don't know if I can promise that," Kenise said. "It depends on how good it is."

"Kenise!" Pam furrowed her brow and glared at her. "If you say one word, I swear I'll have you working weekends till this time next year."

"Fine. I promise not to say a word."

"Okay." Emma closed her eyes and sighed heavily. "Friday, after that lady coded, Mrs. Greene, I ran to the parking lot and cried. When I was there, David came out and tried to cheer me up."

"You mean David the paramedic?" Pam inquired.

"Yes," Emma replied then continued her story. "I was ready to quit and just go home, but he was so nice, he convinced me to come back. Just before I came in… I don't know why I did it."

"Well? Did what?" Kenise pressed again.

"I kissed him."

"Oh, my!" Pam exclaimed with a giggle.

"Really," Kenise gasped. "What did he do?"

Emma shrugged her shoulders. "Well, he kissed back, I think. I'm not sure."

"You're not sure? How can you not be sure? Either he kissed you or he didn't." Kenise kept up her interrogation.

Emma lifted her hands and again shrugged. "Like I said, I'm not sure. He didn't seem to mind it."

"Of course not," Pam smirked. "He's a dirty dog. Taking advantage of you when you're vulnerable. He probably saw you were all upset and went after you like a chicken on a June bug."

"It wasn't like that. He was very sweet." Emma said. David was the perfect gentleman with her, and she couldn't understand why everyone thought of him as a womanizer. He seemed perfectly innocent, and it was she who initiated the kiss.

"I'm sure," Kenise rolled her eyes.

"I suppose neither of us won then," Pam chuckled. "I figured everyone was so out of sorts because David had mouthed off to Dr. Russo again."

"Don't put that money back in your purse yet, missy," Kenise said to Pam. "That doesn't explain why Russo is dragging around here like somebody stole his puppy."

"That's true," Pam agreed. "Kenise bet he walked in on you and David getting handsy in the storage closet."

"Kenise! I would never do something like that at work!" Emma gasped at the suggestion.

"Don't act so insulted. You just owned up to kissing someone at work." Kenise replied. "It's not that far a stretch to think you might have been playing touchy-feeling in the storage room."

"I guess you're right about that." Emma admitted.

"So, you kissed the paramedic and are embarrassed about it. Then what's going on with Dr. Russo?" Pam asked. "Does it have something to do with the Sentinel Event committee?"

"The Sentinel Event? I don't understand. What is that?" Emma asked.

"Oh, I forgot, you left at three Friday, so you didn't hear," Pam said. "Whenever there's an adverse drug reaction it's called a Sentinel Event so Dr. Russo was notified that there will be Root Cause Analysis review."

"You mean, the older lady, Mrs. Greene? Am I going to get fired over it?" Panic filled Emma. She knew she had made a horrible mistake when she gave Mrs. Greene the Lasix, but no one had mentioned the situation since. She thought the matter was over and done.

"No, sweetie," Kenise patted her shoulder to comfort her. "It's a review of what happened. A Root Cause Analysis is just a big name for a chart review. Administration and the medical committee review what happened and then see how we can avoid the problem in the future."

"It was my fault. What if they decide that the best way to avoid the problem is to fire me?" Emma's eyes were red, and she was at the brink of tears.

"Now stop panicking. It's not like that. You're not going to get fired." Pam assured her. "Usually the committee just recommends a change in department policy or the procedure."

"So, you don't think I'll lose my job?"

Kenise gave her a quick hug. "I can't promise anything. Sometimes they recommend disciplinary actions. But I wouldn't go getting all worried about it. Besides, they will probably be harder on Dr. Russo than on you."

"Oh no," Emma said. "I hate that I've gotten him in trouble. Does he know about the review yet?"

"Yes, Sister Faith, told him on Friday." Pam answered.

Emma stiffened up at the news. In the pit of her stomach she ached. "You mean he knew on Friday about the investigation?"

"Uh, yeah," Pam answered. "Sister Faith came by around five, just before he left for the day."

"That bastard!" Emma growled.

Pam and Kenise looked at each other with surprise at Emma's reaction. This was the first time they heard her use any bad language, and Emma seem so innocent. For them it was like seeing a Disney princess curse.

"That explains it. That sorry piece of ---" Emma stopped before finishing and clinched her teeth.

"What is it?" Kenise prodded.

"I went out with friends to a dance club on Saturday night and ran into Finn… Dr. Russo, I mean. He was all over me, being all seductive like a damn snake. He walked me home and tried to get me to invite him to spend the night."

"Nooooo," Kenise and Pam gasped in unison.

"Yes! Of course, I turned him down. Then he asked me out to dinner and showed up at my apartment yesterday wanting to go out. So, I turned him down again."

"Girl, what is your problem? You turned down Dr. Russo?" Pam cried out in disbelief. "Are you out of your mind?"

"I'm glad I did," Emma replied firmly. "He never mentioned a word about the review. I know he was just trying to charm me into covering his despicable butt."

"Are you sure? I can't believe he would be so dirty!" Pam's mouth fell open. How could Emma turn down a man like Russo? Then again, how could Russo be so rotten toward a sweet little thing like Emma? It was mind-boggling.

Kenise shook her head in disbelief. "That is low down."

"He treats me like dirt, insults me at every turn, then suddenly sees me out and wants to hook up? I knew something was wrong the minute he said hello. Thank God I didn't fall for it."

"Girl, what are you going to do?" Kenise asked.

"I'm just going to try to get through the day without punching him in the face." Emma answered.

Suddenly, the door opened and in walked Dr. Russo. All three nurses stiffened up and began rummaging through the supplies pretending to be looking for equipment.

Russo looked at them suspiciously. "Have you made this your personal office now Emma," he asked. "If you're finished with your gossiping, Beds 1 and 5 are ready for discharge instructions and Bed 7 needs transported to the ICU."

"Yes doctor," Kenise answered and quickly darted past him and out the door with Pam right on her heels.

Emma turned and quickly grabbed some supplies from the cart and was preparing to rush out as well, but Finn closed the door and leaned against it to block her exit.

She glared at him. "Can you please move, I have work to do."

"I guess you told everybody about us. What happened, I mean."

"Not everything," Emma said. "But what does it matter? It wasn't anything but a walk. It's not like there was anything real or intimate happened."

"I see. Just so you know, I would prefer in the future if you keep our personal matters private."

"You don't have to worry about that!" Now would you please get out of my way!"

"Emma. Can we talk for just a minute? Is that too much to ask?"

"It depends."

"On what?"

She slammed the supplies she had bundled in her arms down on a nearby cart and looked at him crossly. "Did you, or did you not, know when we ran into each other at the club that there would be a review of Mrs. Greene chart?"

"Sure, I did. It's standard procedure." Finn shrugged indifferently. Whenever there was an adverse drug reaction, there was always a chart review, so he didn't understand why she was upset. "Sister Faith came by and told me Friday it was on the schedule. What about it?"

"That's what I thought! You weren't interested in me were you! You just wanted me to cover your ass."

"Now wait just a minute! You're being ridiculous!"

"Am I?" Emma tried to push passed him, but he did not move and continued to block her exit.

"Yes, you are," he raised his voice at her. "For one thing, why would I need you to cover my ass. You're the one that screwed up!"

Emma tried to push past him, but he wouldn't move. "If you don't get out of my way I'll scream!"

"You mean even louder than you already are?" Finn yelled loudly back at her. He yanked the door open and stepped away. "Go then! If you want to think the worst of me then that's on you, not me."

Emma stormed out and as she did, she almost ran directly into Sister Faith who was giving a tour to a prospective employee. "Oh, excuse me sister," Emma apologized then stormed off down the hallway.

Sister Faith had apparently heard the two yelling at each other in the storage room. She looked directly at Dr. Russo and without changing her expression turned to the applicant and said, "And that, my dear, is the reason I personally discourage employee dating here at St. Rita's." She gave Dr. Russo a stern look then continued her tour.

The rest of the morning Finn and Emma spent avoiding each other as much as possible. They didn't speak or acknowledge each other at all. It was a relief to Emma when Kenise asked her to help transport a patient from the E.R. upstairs to the I.C.U. She was happy for any excuse to get out of Dr. Russo's line of sight. If he ordered her to give one more enema, she was certain she would scream.

Once the patient was settled in his I.C.U. room, Emma asked Kenise if she could take a few moments to check on Mr. Thompson, the trauma patient that had been admitted on her first day of orientation. Kenise readily agreed, happy for the opportunity to stop having to run interference between Emma and Dr. Russo for a little while.

Emma stepped to the sliding glass door of the patient's room and peered inside. He was lying motionless with a small oxygen cannula in his nose. The monitor was silent, displaying a steady heart rate and a rhythmic respiratory wave. He appeared to be resting comfortably.

One of the ICU nurses approached. "Can I help you?"

"Oh, hi," Emma smiled as the woman approached. "I work in the Emergency Department. I was on duty when Mr. Thompson came in and I just wanted to see how he's doing."

"I'm just covering while his nurse is at lunch. She should be back in about 15 minutes if you can wait."

"I'll stop by another time then," Emma replied. She was about to walk away but changed her mind. "Would it be okay if I step inside?"

"I don't see why not. I don't think he is responsive yet. He's breathing on his own and stable, but still hasn't regained consciousness."

"Oh, I see. Well, I'll just stay a moment then."

Emma walked to the bedside and looked down at him. He looked so peaceful, like he was sleeping. She gazed at him for a moment and smiled. He seemed so innocent and nice; she thought. With her hand she gently brushed his hair off his face. Out of nursing habit, she examined the IV that was in his arm. She frowned when she saw that the silk tape around the IV was matted in the thick hair of his forearms. "They should have shaved your arm before putting that tape all over it," she said softly to him. "That's gonna hurt coming off."

She looked at his wristband and read the information. His full name was Michael J. Thompson, and he was 34 years old. Birthdate was August 15. No known allergies. She touched his hand and felt the soft warmth of it. Suddenly, his hand grasped hers and held it.

"I remember you." he said in a weak and raspy voice.

Emma was startled to find that he was awake. "I'm sorry. I didn't mean to disturb you."

"Where am I? How did I get here?" He was confused and getting agitated. The EKG tracing on the heart monitor became faster and it started to sound an alarm.

"Nurse!" Emma called out. "Nurse! Can someone please help!"

The nurse she had spoken with earlier rushed and immediately silenced the monitor alarm.

"Mr. Thompson! You're awake!" She came to the bedside and gently patted him on the arm. "Do you know where you are?"

"Am I in the hospital?" He looked around the room.

"Yes, hon. You're at St. Rita's Catholic Hospital," the nurse answered. "You're in the ICU. Do you remember how you got here?"

"I don't... Uh... I don't remember." He struggled to recall, but the memory eluded him.

"You were in an accident," the nurse informed him. "What's the last thing you remember?"

"I saw her." He looked at Emma.

"I was one of the nurses that took care of you when they brought you into the emergency room." Emma said.

"It was snowing." He said in his confusion.

"Huh?" The comment rattled Emma. Why on earth would he think it had been snowing that day?

"No, Mr. Thompson," the nurse answered as she put a blood pressure cuff on his arm. "It's been a little chilly lately, but we have a long time before we see snow."

He looked up at Emma. "I saw you in the snow. I remember your face."

Emma stepped back from the bedside. What a strange thing for him to say to her. Something about Michael reminded her of Brock, and now this stranger wakes up from a coma and claimed he saw her in the snow. Brock died in her arms on a snow-covered mountain. It was unnerving and uncomfortable for her.

"I've got to go," she said abruptly then ran from the room and down four flights of stairs back to the ER. When she reached the ER, she paused to catch her breath.

Kenise spotted her as she emerged from the stairwell, her face white as if she had seen a ghost. "Girl, what is it? Who'd you kiss this time?"

"No, no." Emma shook her head and looked at Kenise with a confused expression. "That patient, Mr. Thompson. He said the strangest thing."

"Honey, patients say all kinds of strange crap. If I had a dollar for every pervert that asked me for a sponge bath I could retire."

"It wasn't like that." Emma hesitated. She hadn't discussed Brock's death with anyone at work, and she wasn't ready to go down that path.

"What was it? Trust me, I've heard it all."

"It was nothing. Just really odd," Emma brushed it aside. "He said he recognized my face and saw me in the snow."

"So? You were there when they brought him in."

"But why snow?"

"He's a head injury. I wouldn't be surprised if he saw stars," she laughed.

"I guess it's nothing," Emma sighed.

She knew Kenise was probably right. The patient was hallucinating. It was just a random coincidence that the patient saw snow and associated it with her. Because of her own confusion and mixed emotions over Finn, she was grasping for anything she could interpret as a sign of what to do. She wanted to talk to Brock. More importantly she wanted to let him go, but she just didn't know how.

CHAPTER 9

By the end of Emma's second week of orientation she was getting more comfortable with her duties and more confident. She had spent all her free time exploring every inch of the emergency department, learning where the equipment and supplies are kept. She had even read the entire 260 pages of the department policy manual, a feat most of the long-term staff had yet to accomplish.

Although she was much more comfortable finding her way around and locating equipment in a hurry, the situation with Dr. Russo remained as tense as ever. They were still not on speaking terms and exchanged minimal words only when it was absolutely necessary. So, it was unnerving when Sister Faith summoned them both to the administration conference room for interviews with the Root Cause Analysis committee regarding the Mrs. Greene Lasix event.

It had been more than a week since the incident so Emma had forgotten about the review, though it was a mistake she would never forget. It wasn't until Pam approached her with the news that she remembered the Root Cause Analysis investigation.

"Hey, Emma. I need you to give me a quick report on your patients. Sister Faith just called and asked that you go up to the Admin conference room. They're having the RCA review meeting this morning."

"Oh, I forgot about that." Emma was visibly nervous.

"Don't worry. They're just going to review your documentation and probably ask some questions. Be honest and I'm sure it will all be fine."

"I hope so."

"It will," Pam assured her. "Is this your only patient?"

"Yes, it's pretty slow at the moment. He's admitted with a temp of 102 degrees and a sore throat. I did the rapid antigen test, and it confirmed Strep. He's waiting on the doc to write a prescription for antibiotics and then he can be discharged."

"Enjoy the calm while it lasts. Today's Friday and it's a full moon. The crazies will start early today."

"Okay, thanks Pam."

When Emma arrived in Administration, a secretary was waiting to escort her to the conference room where the RCA meeting was already in progress. She swallowed hard as she glanced around the room at the committee members in their professional business attire with their matter-of-fact expressions.

"Miss Paige, thank you for coming," Sister Faith stood and welcomed her. "Please have a seat."

"Thank you." Emma found an empty chair at the long conference table and melted into it hoping to go unnoticed.

"Miss Paige, we haven't met yet," a silver haired, stern man addressed her from the head of the table. "I'm Dr. Morgan, the Emergency Room Medical Director. Welcome to St. Rita's. I trust you are settling in well?"

"Yes, I'm getting into the routine; that is, if there is anything routine in the emergency room."

"That's good. Have you met everyone here?" Morgan asked.

"I'm sorry. I've only been here two weeks so unless I've given you an enema in the emergency room, then we haven't met," she laughed nervously.

"Let's go around the table and introduce ourselves before we begin. I see one or two new faces this morning myself." Dr. Morgan said.

Seated to Dr. Morgan's right was Sister Faith. She smiled brightly and looked around the table. "I think I know everyone, and everyone knows me, but just in case I'm Sister Faith. I'm an assistant Administrator."

"I'm Sandra Rose, the Director of Nursing." A woman dressed in a business pant suit said.

Emma already knew her. Sandra was the one who interviewed her and ultimately offered her the job. Emma slumped down in the chair slightly. She was embarrassed to be seeing Mrs. Rose under these circumstances after she had worked so hard to convince her she was ready and qualified for the job. She cringed as she wondered if Mrs. Rose now regretted hiring her.

Finn spoke up, "I'm Doctor Russo. I'm the emergency department physician who was treating Mrs. Greene at the time of the adverse drug reaction."

Emma and Finn looked at each other and he gave her a slight smile. Despite their tense relationship it was comforting for her to see him there. She didn't know if he would throw her under the bus, still it was nice to see him smile even if he was about to pull the rug out from under her.

The introductions continued around the table, one after the other, until everyone had said their names, none of which Emma could remember. There were eight participants; Dr.'s Morgan and Russo, Sister Faith, Sandra Rose, Amanda from Risk Management, a staff pharmacist, and two ER staff nurses who worked the night shift. Everyone seemed rather friendly and non-threatening, so Emma relaxed slightly after the introductions.

"Shall we begin," Sister Faith took control of the room. "Emma, I assume this is your first experience with the RCA process?"

"Yes, ma'am. It is."

"Just briefly, Amanda will you explain what an RCA is and our purpose." Sister Faith addressed the Risk Management representative, Amanda.

Amanda was a tall woman with short gray hair and thin features. Her glasses rested on the tip of her nose as she looked down at her clipboard and began to read from it.

"RCA is the acronym for Root Cause Analysis. The RCA is a facilitated team process to identify the root cause or causes of an event that resulted in an undesired outcome and develop corrective actions. The RCA process provides a means to identify failures in processes or systems that contributed to the undesired outcome and helps establish a plan to prevent future events. The purpose of an RCA is to find out what happened, why it happened, and determine what changes need to be made. The RCA is not a disciplinary process though it can be an early step in an employee Performance Improvement Plan. Its primary aim is to identify what breakdowns in procedures and systems contributed to the undesired outcome and how to prevent ---."

"Thank you, Amanda." Sister Faith interrupted to everyone's relief. It was clear that Amanda intended to read the entire stack of papers on her clipboard and Sister Faith was not about to let that happen.

"To put it simply, we had an adverse drug reaction in the Emergency Department several days ago which qualifies as a Sentinel Event." Dr. Morgan spoke up. He had been tapping his pen on the table, already impatient with the process. "The team has reviewed the medical records and conducted a review of the documentation. We'd just like to her first hand from the treating care team what transpired."

"Yes," Sister Faith agreed. "We know the details of the event and the committee has reviewed the medical records. The purpose of today's meeting is so we can hear directly from the care team what transpired."

"I see." Emma said, but she really didn't see. RCA? Sentinel Event? Joint Commission? Those were all vague, but familiar terms and when they were all grouped together in one sentence, it seemed very intimidating. Rather than risk appearing unprepared and under qualified, she decided to nod her head and keep silent.

"Well, why don't we start with you Dr. Russo," Sister Faith asked. "You were the treating physician for the patient?"

"That's correct," Finn answered. "You can see my notes in the chart regarding the patient's admission and treatment course. I would assume you are only interested in the events specific to the adverse drug reaction."

Sister Faith nodded. "If you can give a brief verbal account of the events leading up to the Code Blue that would be great."

"Sure. Mrs. Greene arrived at the emergency room by ambulance. She had a history of Chronic CHF and was on maintenance doses of the usual ACE inhibitors, Beta blockers, and diuretics. According to her admission report she ran out of her meds several days prior and had missed multiple days of therapy."

"I know Mrs. Greene," one of the staff nurses interjected. "She has trouble getting to and from the pharmacy to get her prescriptions. I would lay odds that before she ran out, she was already cutting her pills in half to make them last longer."

"That's a shame," the pharmacist added. "I can find out her local pharmacy and see if they will deliver to her instead of having to miss doses."

"That would be great if you could work something out for her," the staff nurse agreed.

"That would be helpful, I'm sure." Sister Faith jotted the suggestion down on her notepad. "If you can look into that and report back to the committee that would be great."

"To continue," Finn pressed on. "I was with another patient at the time Mrs. Greene came in, so Emma admitted her and performed an initial assessment in my absence."

"Is that standard practice for nurses to admit patients?" Amanda peered over her glasses in judgement.

"It is," Finn responded with a facial expression and tone of voice that just stopped short of calling her an idiot. "It is an emergency room. Doctors can't be present for every admission. That is why we have nurses, isn't it?"

Amanda sat back in her chair like a scolded dog. "I'm sorry, it's been a long time since I worked patient care. I just wanted to know what the standard of care is."

"Unless the patient is unstable, the nurse will admit and do the initial assessment." Finn explained, this time a little more gently. "Once the nurse has seen the patient, she will let the doctor know and give me a report. That way patients are triaged and seen according to medical needs and available resources."

"Patients get triaged twice," one of the night nurses offered further clarification. "When they present to the ER a triage nurse evaluates every patient. Then once they're in a treatment room, the assigned nurse performs a more detailed assessment and notify the docs."

"I understand," Amanda answered. "Sorry to interrupt."

"Going on," Finn resumed. "I was busy with another patient at the time of Mrs. Greene's admission, so the nurse admitted her. After her evaluation Nurse Paige advised me that Mrs. Greene was exhibiting signs of shortness of breath with edema. She gave a brief patient history. After hearing the report, I gave a verbal order to administer 40 mg of Lasix. By the time I finished with the patient, I heard a Code Blue announced. I ran to the treatment room to find Miss Paige had already begun CPR and the code team was arriving."

"I have a few questions regarding the Lasix order," Dr. Morgan said. "So, when you gave the verbal order, was there any question of allergies or concerns about giving Lasix? That is what caused the arrest, wasn't it? The patient had an allergic reaction?"

"Yes. The patient went into anaphylactic shock shortly after receiving the Lasix," Russo answered. "As far as known drug allergies, we didn't have the complete medical record at the time, but she did have an allergy alert armband that indicated the patient was allergic to Bactrim."

"That's odd," the pharmacist noted. "Bactrim is a sulfa-class medication so the armband should have said that rather than the just Bactrim."

"Lasix is a sulfa drug?" Sister Faith asked.

"Yes, it has a sulfur-based component," the pharmacist answered. "So, if someone is allergic to Bactrim which is a sulfa-class antibiotic, there's a strong likelihood for cross sensitivity to Lasix as well."

"So, the allergy alert band was improperly labeled?" Mrs. Rose asked. "Is that my understanding?"

"I wouldn't say it was improperly labeled," Dr. Morgan replied. "I'd say it was inadequately labeled. Most doctors and RN's should know that if a patient is allergic to Bactrim that they should not have Lasix either."

"I didn't know that," one of the night nurses volunteered.

"So, were you aware that the patient was allergic to Bactrim when you gave the verbal order for Lasix?" Dr. Morgan asked Dr. Russo.

Finn glanced at Emma but hesitated to respond. He was reluctant to appear that he was trying to pass the blame off to Emma. No matter, how angry and hurt he was, he didn't intend to implicate her.

"Dr. Russo?" Morgan pressed for the answer.

"Yes, I believe Nurse Paige told me the patient was allergic to Bactrim," Dr. Russo lied. He knew that was not the case. Emma had said nothing about patient allergies; in fact, he had specifically told her to check.

Emma audibly gasped at what he said. Rather than tossing her under the bus as she had expected, Finn was instead lying to protect her. She suddenly felt ashamed of herself for being so mean to him and jumping to conclusions. This was not his fault and she would not let him take the blame for her mistakes, even if it meant losing her job.

"That's not completely accurate." Emma shook her head.

"Oh?" Sister Faith raised her eyebrows in curiosity.

"No Sister," Emma said. "Dr. Russo is not at fault. The blame rests solely with me. When I spoke with Dr. Russo and took the verbal order, he specifically told me to check the patient's allergies before administering the Lasix. I checked the patient's alert bracelet and saw she was allergic to Bactrim. At the time I didn't know Lasix was a sulfa medication, and I didn't know there was a cross sensitivity between Sulfa antibiotics and Lasix. So, it was completely my fault and I take full responsibility for the error."

"Is that true, Dr. Russo?" Sister Faith asked.

"I suppose it is." He bit his lower lip and looked down at the table. "In all fairness, I gave the order, so it was my responsibility."

Sister Faith slightly laughed. "I appreciate your candor, both of you. And it's admirable that you are so willing to accept blame. But the purpose of this review is not to divvy out blame, it is to determine where the process broke down and how we can prevent it in from happening again."

"Seems there was a combination of issues that contributed to the error," Dr. Morgan noted. "The patient's old chart was not available. The allergy alert wristband was inadequately labeled. And then there's the issue of staff education as to cross sensitivity with sulfa-class drugs."

From that point in the meeting Emma zoned out. The committee continued to discuss how the event with Mrs. Greene could have been prevented and how they would investigate better ways to label armbands. The pharmacist volunteered to provide additional training to the staff regarding drug allergies. Emma paid little attention to the discussion from there forward. It was just such a relief to know that her head was not on the chopping block.

After what seemed like an eternity, the meeting finally adjourned. Emma hurried out the room not sure what, if anything, had been resolved. Her only certainty was that she was not getting fired, and more importantly, she had greatly misjudged Finn. She was ashamed for the way she had accused him and knew she had to apologize.

Emma waited inside the stairwell knowing that would be the way Finn would go heading back to the emergency room. After a little while the door opened, and Finn entered.

"What are you doing here?" He jumped slightly when he found her lurking in the stairwell.

"I wanted to catch you before you went back to the department," she answered. "I owe you an apology and didn't want to wait. I really misjudged you, didn't I?"

"No harm, no foul." He brushed it off and walked past her and started down the stairs.

She hoped he would take a moment to talk with her, but he didn't. She couldn't blame him after the things she had said and the way she behaved.

"Thank you!" She called after him. "You didn't have to do that for me."

"I didn't do it for you," he said as he continued his descent. "This hospital needs good nurses."

"Is that the only reason?"

"Yes, it is."

She heard him push the exit door open and then it slammed shut behind him. She smiled. She knew the truth even if he wouldn't admit it.

Chapter 10

Steadily over the next few days, the tension between Emma and Finn began to thaw. After the incident in the RCA review, she saw him in a completely different light. Rather than thinking of him as an arrogant jerk impossible to please, she saw him for what he truly was, a perfectionist with a strict work ethic. Whenever he spoke harshly to her, she resisted the impulse to take it personally; instead, she accepted his disapproval as constructive criticism.

Finn, on the other hand, attempted to curtail his disparaging remarks, not just of Emma, but to the entire staff. Because of his fall-out with Emma, he suddenly recognized that he had been a tyrant with the staff and that he had a reputation for being unreasonable. Until Emma confronted him, no one had dared to say it to his face; and when Emma finally did, it stung him deeply. He wanted to be a great doctor, and he finally realized that to be a great doctor he also needed to be a great team player. He continued to drop insults from time to time out of habit, but he would almost immediately apologize when he did.

One incident happened when they were treating a combative patient. Pam and Kenise were struggling to hold the patient down while Dr. Russo attempted to start an IV in his arm. Just as Dr. Russo inserted the needle into the patient's forearm, Pam lost her grip and the patient hit Finn in the stomach. Instantly, Russo filled the room with a fog of expletives.

Once the IV was finally in place and secured, Finn left the room while the nurses remained to give sedation and to place the patient in restraints. A few moments later, Russo popped back in the doorway.

"Pam," he said. "I apologize for yelling at you earlier, it was uncalled for. The guy's jacked up on something and strong as an ox. It wasn't your fault."

Pam eyes widened in surprise and her mouth dropped open. Having never heard Dr. Russo apologize before she didn't know how to respond. She just stood there gawking at him in silence.

"Are we good?" Russo asked.

"Sure. No worries."

Finn flashed a brief smile then disappeared back down the hallway. The ladies looked at each other in disbelief.

"He's dying," Pam pronounced. "He's dying and afraid he's going to hell for the way he's acted. There's no other explanation I can think of."

"Maybe he's found Jesus," Kenise laughed.

"More like he's found administration. I bet someone complained and Sister Faith put the fear of God in him."

"People have complained before and it didn't make a bit of difference. No, something has happened to give him an epiphany."

"Or maybe he's finally getting laid," Pam cackled. "You think he and Emma are seeing each other on the sly?"

"I think she's more interested in David. They seem to spend a lot of their lunches and breaks together lately."

"I'm pretty sure Emma busted his ego when he tried to date her. Maybe he's trying to turn over a new leaf."

"Remind me to send her a thank-you card then, because it sure is peaceful lately," Kenise added.

It was true that Emma was spending a lot of her time on break chatting with David. They had quickly become thick as thieves, spending all their breaks together and frequently taking their lunches together in the break room. In truth, there was nothing romantic between them despite all the whispers and gossip. Emma found David very attractive, and he was drawn to her as well; but so far, the attraction was nothing beyond friendship.

There was another man that was occupying just as many of her breaks as David was. Emma had become close to Michael Thompson, her first trauma patient. She checked on him frequently and before long they had become close friends.

In fact, while Pam and Kenise were fighting with the combative patient, Emma was in the step-down unit visiting Michael during her break.

"What did you get for lunch?" Emma lifted the cover off Michael's lunch tray and crinkled her nose at the liver and onions she discovered underneath. "Surely you didn't order that?"

"I sure did," he said and grinned. "I love liver and onions. Hopefully, the hospital cafeteria won't ruin it for me."

Emma opened his packet of plastic-ware and organized his lunch tray then moved the table so he could eat. "I've never met anyone who actually liked liver."

"You've not met many quality men then have you? I could eat my weight in liver if it's cooked right."

"If that is the acid test for a quality man, then I guess I haven't."

Michael picked up a piece of liver and took a bite and began to chew very slowly like he was relishing it. "Mmmm."

"How is it?" Emma again crinkled her nose and grimaced.

"It's good for hospital food. Care for a taste?"

"Heck no!"

He cut another small piece with some onion and picked it up with his fork. "Aw, come on. Live a little."

"I'd hate to throw up on you."

"Have you ever tried it?"

"I can't say that I have, nor do I want to."

"Ah come on. Take a risk. How can you say you don't like something you've never tried?" He pushed the fork toward her mouth. "Just a little taste."

Michael put the fork to his mouth then pretended to take a bite. "Yum, yum, yum," he said and pretended to chew. "See. Uncle Mikey likes it," he continued as if speaking to a child.

"Oh, stop it!" She giggled.

She stared at the dark brown meat on his fork along with a limp onion hanging down from it. It looked like a rancid piece of meat and the onion reminded her of some intestinal parasite she's seen in her medical books.

"Just one little bite," he insisted and edged the liver closer to her mouth.

"All right, all right! One bite. And if I throw up, I'm aiming at you."

Reluctantly Emma closed her eyes tightly and opened her mouth. He gently placed the fork in her mouth and she took the chunk of liver and began to chew, slowly. She opened her eyes and tilted her head. Her mouth curled into a very slight smile and she nodded her approval.

"Well, was I right? Or was I right?" He asked with great satisfaction.

"Okay," she said after she swallowed it down. "I'll admit, it wasn't half bad."

"Remember, it's hospital food. My mamma makes it a lot better."

"I think I could eat it if I was starving, but it's not something I'll ever intentionally order off a menu."

Michael happily continued his lunch. He ate like he was famished, cutting big chunks of the liver then scooping up the onions before shoveling in his mouth. Emma watched with amusement at how much he enjoyed his lunch. She loved how the muscles in his cheeks flexed as he chewed, she'd never noticed that with any other man.

"So, how's your day going?" Michael took a break from chewing to ask.

"It's a little slow but will probably pick up this afternoon. We get a lot of chest pain patients right after the buffet closes across the street." She wasn't making a joke although it may have sounded like one. The fact was that right after the all-you-can-eat buffet closed in the afternoon, a rush of seniors complaining of chest pain would arrive in the ER.

"Hey, I heard you may go home in a couple more days." Emma remembered hearing that Michael was well on his way to being discharged.

"That's what they tell me. Can you believe it? I come in here with my head cracked open and my heart busted like an old radiator. I'm a lucky man to be able to walk out of here."

"You certainly are. I think you know how close you came to dying." Although she was catholic Emma wasn't very religious, but if she ever saw a miracle, Michael was the one.

"I'm glad I don't remember any of that. I'm pretty sure I didn't see a white light or a tunnel, so either God wasn't ready for me yet or I was going to the other place."

"Say, Michael. I've meant to ask you something."

"What's that?"

"When you woke up in ICU, you said you remembered my face and that you saw me in the snow. What did you mean?"

"Did I? I don't remember that." He tried to recollect, but the memory was too vague for him to recall.

"Have you seen me somewhere before?"

"No, I'm sure of that. I would remember that smile anywhere.

She was disappointed. She had hoped that there was some meaning to what he had said. That somehow Brock had reached out to her through Michael. It seemed like a foolish notion to her now; obviously it was only Michael's confusion and pain medications.

Just then Emma's phone made a chirp. She read the message displayed on the screen aloud. "Code Grey. Emergency Waiting Room."

"What's a Code Grey?"

"Good question." Emma flipped over her name badge to scan the list of codes she had printed out and taped to the back.

"Oh, I have to run," she announced and headed to the door.

"What going on?"

"It's a security code. Must be a fight or something. I better get down there. You enjoy your liver."

"Thanks! You go enjoy your fight," he laughed as she hurried out the door. "Remember, sting like a bee."

Chapter 11

Emma wasn't sure what her duties were during a Code Grey, but she knew if there was a disturbance, she needed to be on hand to help as needed. She rushed down the stairway and burst through the door that opened into the back hallway of the Emergency Department. She didn't immediately see anyone, but she heard shouting emanating from where she believed to be the front lobby of the Emergency Department.

She ran toward the commotion and when she rounded the corner, she saw a crowd gathered at the double doors leading to the lobby.

"What's happening?" Emma asked when she reached the group.

"There was a meeting of the gun and knife club. When they brought the victims in, their friends followed and started brawling in the waiting room."

"Oh, crap!" Emma said. "Is security out there."

"Yeah, security ran them all out into the parking lot and the police are on the way." Another staff person answered.

As if there wasn't already enough commotion going on, the Code Blue alarm sounded in a nearby trauma room. Emma and several of the other staff raced toward the trauma room where the blue light was flashing above the door. Inside she found David performing chest compressions while Dr. Russo was at the head of the bed intubating the patient.

"Tube's in," Finn said. He immediately connected it to the resuscitation bag and began rhythmically squeezing it to deliver breaths. "End tidal confirms CO2. Can somebody listen for breath sounds?"

Kenise ran to the bedside and began listening to the patient's chest. After a moment, "Bilateral and equal," she announced.

Emma hurried to the bedside. "What can I do?"

"Relieve David for a few cycles," Finn instructed.

David stopped compressions and stepped off the stool and backed away so that she could take his place. He was dripping with sweat from performing CPR and was glad for the relief.

"Are you all right?" It concerned Emma when she saw his arms and shirt were blood-stained.

"Yeah, I'm fine; not my blood. He was spewing from his gut when we arrived on the scene."

Emma jumped up on the stool, placed her hands on the center of the patient's chest and restarted compressions. The patient's abdomen had a large amount of blood-soaked gauze and with each compression blood oozed from around the dressing and poured on the stretcher.

No sooner had Emma begun CPR that Dr. Russo announced, "Ok, let's call it. Time of death, 1:15 p.m."

"Oh, hell nah!" A male voice demanded.

Everyone turned to see a young man push his way through the group of onlookers that hovered outside the door. He was no more than 16 or 17 years old, wearing a dingy white t-shirt with his pants sagging so low to reveal the entire length of his boxer shorts.

He was a typical street thug, or at least he was trying to be as he aggressively forced his way into the room, flinging his arms in the air. Nobody was afraid, instead when he strutted in acting all gangster-like Kenise openly laughed.

"Wha' you laughing at bitch?" He spat the words out.

David quickly positioned himself to block the boy from approaching the trauma team. "Son, you need to get back to the waiting room. Someone will come to talk to you shortly."

"Nah, man! I ain't your son, and I ain't going nowhere." He attempted to push past, but David continued to block him. The boy pointed at Dr. Russo and said, "You fix'm. If he dies you die. You hear me, motha fuka? If he dies, you die!"

"Somebody call security," Kenise called out to the staff standing in the doorway.

"I got him," David approached him. "Come on man, you need to step back outside."

The kid pushed David hard in the chest then raised his fists. "Come on," he taunted David and assumed a boxer stance. "Come at me old man."

David had no patience left for the kid. He grabbed the boy by the arm and twisted it behind his back so quickly that the kid was crying out in pain before he could even react.

"Don't touch me!" The boy shouted. "Don't put your hands on me!"

"You listen to me you little punk." David growled in the kid's ear. "If you don't calm your ass down, I'm going to break your arm off and beat you with it. Do you understand?"

"Yes," the boy moaned.

David released his grip and let the kid loose. When he did, the boy pulled a knife from under his jacket and plunged it into David's side. There was a collective gasp from everyone in the room and then several nurses including Emma screamed.

The boy stepped back as David fell to his knees, clutching at his side and groaning. When the boy realized what he had done, he dropped the knife to the floor and ran out of the trauma room and out of the hospital.

Emma ran to David. "Are you okay? How bad is it?"

"Well—," David groaned in pain. "Let's say I've been better."

"Get a stretcher in here," Russo ordered and rushed to David. He quickly ripped open David's shirt and examined the wound; it was bleeding profusely.

"I'm going to help you lay flat, do you think you can do that?" Finn braced one arm against David's back to help support his weight.

"As long as you promise not to let me die on this nasty floor," David laughed and immediately cried out in pain.

"Ok, funny man," Russo said. "I need you to lay back."

Emma positioned herself on the opposite side as Finn and together they supported his back together they slowly eased him flat onto the floor.

Dr. Russo examined the wound again, this time more closely. As he gently touched around the puncture David groaned loudly.

"How bad is it?" David asked.

"It's a clean entry, about two inches wide," Finn told him. He turned to Emma, "I need some sterile gauze to hold pressure."

Someone passed Emma a stack of gauze pads and she quickly tore open the packages and handed the pads to Finn. He placed them on the wound and held pressure to control the bleeding.

"Kenise, call the O.R. Tell them we need a room and a surgical team scrubbed and ready to go STAT. Emma, I need you to hold pressure for me."

Finn grabbed Emma's hand and placed it onto the mound of bloody gauze on David's abdomen. "Not too much pressure, just enough to stop the oozing."

"Surgery?" David didn't like the sound of that. He attempted to raise up and check out the wound himself, but the pain made him drop back on the floor. "You can't be serious. Just stitch me up and call it a day."

"Well, buddy. You're still bleeding, and I'm concerned about your liver."

"I had paper cuts in Nam that was worse than this," David joked nervously.

"I didn't know you were in Vietnam." Emma said.

"It was a joke! Just how old do you think I am, Emma?" David laughed but immediately regretted his attempt at humor when another wave of pain swept through his side.

Kenise returned to the room. "O.R. will be ready for him in five. The surgical team is scrubbing."

Within minutes David was on a stretcher headed to the operating room. Emma stayed with him, holding his hand the entire way.

"Listen. You'll be fine." Emma reassured him. "Is there anything you need me to do? Anybody I should call?"

"Yeah, if you don't mind, make sure someone calls my house. Joe needs to know what's going on."

"I'll make sure," Emma promised.

CHAPTER 12

Emma checked her watch again; it had only been two minutes since the last time she had checked. Time was dragging, and the wait was excruciating for her. She jumped up from the sofa and paced back and forth in the empty waiting room. It had been over two hours since they took David into surgery, and still there was no word.

It was after five o'clock and there were no scheduled surgeries, so the waiting room was empty except for Emma. That made the time pass even slower. There was nothing to distract her attention, no one to speak to, no people to watch; it was just her and her growing anxiety. She was so relieved when Finn walked in, she ran up to him and hugged him. After the brief embrace Emma stepped back, embarrassed that she had done so.

"I'm sorry," she said. "I'm just so worried."

"It's quite all right," Finn replied. He was glad to have her in his arms if only for a moment. "Any word?"

"Not yet."

Finn looked at his watch. "It's not been that long; I wouldn't be too worried just yet. I'm sure he's going to be fine."

"I'm certain of it, but this waiting is horrible."

"Oh, I almost forgot." Finn handed her a neatly folded set of blue scrubs. "I thought you might like to change."

Emma looked down at her uniform dress and for the first time saw it was splattered with dried blood. "Oh lord. I never even noticed. Thanks."

"I hope I got the right size."

"There is no right size when it comes to scrubs. One size fits none, and nobody looks good in them." She accepted the bundle of clothes and gave a half smile. "But I do appreciate you bringing them."

"There's a restroom around the corner. Go change, and I'll hang out here in case there's any news."

"You don't need to do that."

"No, I don't, but I want to. I'm worried about him too."

"Okay, I'll just be a minute," Emma said then headed off to the restroom to change.

A few minutes later she returned dressed in the scrubs. They fit her perfectly and despite her earlier remark; the scrubs were very flattering to her figure.

"You were wrong," Finn said when he saw her.

"About what?"

"You said nobody looked good in scrubs. Guess you're the exception." He smiled and gave her a once-over. "David is a very lucky man."

"Thank you." Emma's eyes widened when she realized what he had just said. "What do you mean, David's a very lucky man? You think we're together?"

"Aren't you? The whole hospital is talking about it. And here you are pacing the floor over him. I mean, it is pretty obvious you're a couple."

"No, we're not. We're just good friends." It surprised Emma that he would think she was dating David. Although she had entertained that possibility when they first met, she and David had moved into the friend zone rather quickly. He was the handsome, rugged type she liked, but things just seemed more natural for them as close friends. She couldn't figure out why there was no chemistry between them, but whatever the reason, she was thrilled with their relationship as it was.

"I thought—, but you guys—."

"Is that why you've been avoiding me?"

"I wasn't avoiding you. I just didn't want to cause problems between you two."

She smiled brightly at him. "You could've asked."

"Wasn't my business for one thing, and for another you know how I feel about bringing personal matters into work."

"For your information, I'm not seeing David nor anyone else at the moment." She didn't know how much clearer she could make it.

"I suspected as much. There's no way you could kiss me the way you did and get over it that quickly." His eyes sparkled as if he was about to laugh.

"Oh really? You think you're that good?" She laughed at him, but in all honesty, he really was that good. She knew it. No one has every kissed her like he did on the street that night when he walked her home. No kiss had ever felt so passionate to her, so perfect as with Finn. She couldn't deny it to herself, but for the time being, she intended to deny him to satisfaction of knowing the truth.

He grinned. "Well, I'd like to think so."

Emma took a seat across from him. "Keep thinking that if it helps you get through those lonely nights."

A young man rushed into the waiting room; he was out of breath from running up the stairs. He looked to be in his early 30's, clean cut, professional and dressed in a business suit and tie.

"I'm looking for the surgery waiting room." He said to Emma and Finn as he tried to catch his breath.

"This is it," Emma answered. "Are you by chance Joe?"

"Yeah, Joe Branham. You are?"

"I'm Emma Paige. I'm one of the ER nurses. I work with David."

"Oh, okay. Is David all right? They told me downstairs he was in surgery."

"There hasn't been any word yet, we're still waiting. Why don't you sit down and catch your breath, it shouldn't be much longer."

Joe sat in one of the chairs and stared at the closed operating room doors. From his expression, it was clear he was distraught with worry. Every few seconds, Joe would rub his eyes and sniff as if he were fighting back tears.

Emma sat back on the sofa beside Finn. "He looks really upset." She whispered to Finn. "They must be very close."

Finn looked at her with wide eyes and raised his eyebrows. "You really don't get it?"

"Get what?"

"That's David's lover." He whispered.

"It is not." She jabbed him in the side with her elbow. "That's his roommate."

"Right." Finn leaned over and buried his face in his hands and snickered. "Men in their mid-30s don't have roommates unless they're just out of prison or rehab."

"Stop joking, Finn. It's neither the time nor the place."

"I'll bet you dinner it's his boyfriend."

"I'll take that bet, because I know he's not gay." She whispered. "And don't think I'll let you get by with McDonald's or the hospital cafeteria either."

"Neither will you."

Dr. Russo stepped over to where Joe sat biting on his thumb. "Hello, I'm Finn Russo I'm one of the emergency room physicians.

David and I've worked together for several years now. He's a great guy."

Finn extended his hand, and they shook warmly.

"Thanks. It's good to meet you finally. I've heard a lot about you." Joe replied.

"Not all bad, I hope."

"No, not at all. David doesn't say anything bad about anybody."

Emma walked over to join them. "That's true. He always has something nice to say about everybody."

"That's how David is," Joe smiled back. "I'm sorry if I was so distant earlier. With what's going on I'm really scattered right now."

"No worries, I understand it's difficult. You have a right to be scattered and distracted." Emma assure him.

"Do either of you know exactly what happened? When the nurse called, she said a patient had stabbed him. She didn't give any details. I was on the other side of the city, so it took me a while to get here."

"Actually, Emma and I were both there," Finn answered. "We were treating several victims of a gang fight and unfortunately we lost one. One of his friends became aggressive and threatened the staff.

David tried to get the guy to leave the room and before anyone knew it, the kid pulled out a knife and stabbed David."

"He was alert and joking when they took him to surgery," Emma added. "He was trying not to show it, but he was in a lot of pain."

"Sounds like him," Joe said. "So, he wasn't hurt that badly then?"

"It was pretty deep," Finn answered. "With a deep stab wound we don't know what internal damage there may have been. That's why he's in surgery, to check for internal damage."

"Okay, I see." Joe looked down at the floor in contemplation.

"David's a pretty private person here at work," Finn began his fishing expedition. "It's great to meet you finally, I'm just sorry it's under these circumstances."

"Same here. It's nice to match the names with faces," Joe replied. "I've heard so much about everybody, I feel like I know everyone already."

"I can imagine. So how long have you guys been together?" Finn's question was blunt, but he asked in such a casual manner that it didn't seem so intrusive. Emma's mouth dropped open at the audacity of the question, but Joe didn't seem offended.

"Actually, I didn't know he talked to anyone at work about us."

"He keeps his personal life quiet for the most part." Finn intentionally avoided admitting that David never spoke to him about his sexuality.

"He doesn't want to be out at work. He's afraid how some of the guys will treat him if they find out."

"I understand. Some people are still living in the dark ages, but between you and me, I think he's really being overly cautious. Medical people are more open-minded than the general public. I don't think anyone would at the hospital would have a problem with it."

"That's what I keep telling him."

Emma listened in quiet awe as Finn skillfully extracted information from Joe. Finn had a knack for small talk, and his charisma could make a priest gush with all his secrets. As she listened to the conversation, it suddenly occurred to her that Finn was no longer prying. He wasn't being nosey or judgmental; he was being nice to Joe who desperately needed a friend at that moment.

Emma never suspected during all the flirting and teasing that exchanged between them that David was gay and had a lover. And there was the kiss. Emma felt horrible when she recalled kissing David in the parking lot. She thought he must have been appalled by her taking such liberties with him. But in all fairness, he did kiss her back and didn't seem to have any complaints when it happened.

"So how long have you guys been together?" Finn asked again.

"Almost seven years. We were stationed together in Afghanistan and one thing led to another. Once we were out of the service, we got married. It'll be three years this November."

"Really? Three years," Finn repeated. "That would be around the time he started work here, wouldn't it?"

"It was. He proposed right after he started, and we went to the courthouse and got married when he got his first paycheck. I hadn't landed a job yet, and didn't know a lot of people, so we decided to do it on the cheap."

"It's a shame he didn't feel like he could invite some of us from work. I would have loved to have attended. But I understand him being private about it all."

They were interrupted by the double doors to the surgical suit swinging open and a man in light green scrubs emerged.

"David Marshall's family?" He asked as he approached them.

"I'm his husband," Joe stood and replied.

"I'm Dr. Pettiway. I'm Mr. Marshall's surgeon."

"How is he?"

"He's stable, and we can expect a full recovery. The blade lacerated the right posterior lobe of his liver, but luckily, it missed the major blood vessels. As far as knife wounds go, it could have been much worse. A few inches to the left and it could have been life threatening."

"So, he's gonna be all right?" Joe asked again.

"He'll be as good as new in a couple of weeks." Pettiway assured him.

"Thank God," Emma grabbed Finn by the hand. She was so relieved her eyes began to tear up.

"When can I see him?" Joe asked.

"He's in recovery and is awake, but still a little groggy from the anesthesia. But I can take you back now."

"Great, thanks," Joe answered. He paused and looked at Finn and Emma. "Did you want to see him?"

"We'll check on him later," Finn answered. "I'm sure there's only one person he wants to see right now."

"Just let him know we were here," Emma added. "And if he needs anything, he has my number. If either of you need anything, really, please call me."

"Thank you, I appreciate that." Joe said.

Joe followed Dr. Pettiway back through the double doors toward the recovery room. Once they were gone, Emma picked up her blood-stained nursing uniform and prepared to leave.

"I guess I'll see you tomorrow." Emma said.

"I'm off tomorrow." Finn answered.

"But tomorrow's Thursday." She was disappointed. Now that they were on good terms, she looked forward to working with him.

"I need to run some errands. Renew my driver's license, pay bills. Mundane stuff like that."

"Then I guess I'll see you on Friday."

"Yeah, Friday," Finn answered. "If you're heading out now, I'll walk down with you. I'm sure Kenise has been clamoring for me since I've been gone."

They headed down the back stairs into the Emergency Room. Just as Finn had predicted Kenise was running the hallway calling his name.

"Dr. Russo, you have a twisted ankle in Room 4, gastric pain in Room 6, and a nausea and vomiting in Room 10." Kenise spoke rapidly as she ran past him to another patient room. Then she added, "Nice scrubs, Emma. You look like a real nurse now."

"I'm on it," Finn called after her. He turned back to Emma. "See, the scrubs are working for you."

She looked at the blood-stained uniform in her arm. "This is the third uniform I've ruined this month. You just can't get blood out of whites. I guess I need to give up and go to scrubs."

"See, I was right again. You need to learn to follow doctor's orders."

"You were right, this time at least." She smiled. "Well, I'm heading home. There's a hot bubble bath calling my name."

She turned and walked down the hall toward the exit.

"Hey, Emma!" Finn hurried to catch up with her. "Listen. About David and his friend. I mean his husband."

"What about them?"

"Don't say anything about it." Finn lowered his voice so as not to be overheard. "You know, let him share that in his own time."

"Of course," Emma agreed. She was relieved that Finn would ask her to respect David's privacy. He was more compassionate than she had thought. Finn was a beautiful man, but she was beginning to realize his true beauty lay not in his physical features; the most beautiful part was what lay hidden inside.

CHAPTER 13

"Hey, good looking! You up for a visitor?" Emma peeked through the door of his hospital room. She had impatiently waited for her first morning break to run up to his room to check on him.

"Hey, you! Get in here." He beamed as she walked in. "Of course, I'm always up for a visit from my second favorite girl."

She went to his bedside and grabbed his hand and held it affectionately. "Your second?" She contorted her mouth into an exaggerated fake pout. "Who's replaced me. Tell me the skank's name."

David laughed then grabbed his side in pain. "Sorry, but mom is number one."

"In that case, you're forgiven," Emma smiled. "And sorry about that skank comment."

"It's all right." David leaned toward her and whispered. "Truth be told, she can be one at times."

"How you feelin?"

"Really sore. I think the surgery was worse than being stabbed. Apparently, the doc had to stitch up my liver and tie off a couple blood vessels. I'm not gonna complain, it could be much worse."

"That's what the surgeon said last night. You were lucky the knife wasn't a tad to the left."

"Actually, if I was lucky, I wouldn't have been shanked by a wannabe thug in the first place."

"What were you thinking going after that guy anyway?" Emma scolded him as she took a seat next to his bed.

"He was just a kid. I didn't think he would have a blade until he stuck me with it."

"I heard the cops haven't found him yet," Emma said. "He's probably out of the state by now."

"He better hope the cops find him before I do," David said in a serious voice than made Emma worried he might go looking for the punk.

"You leave that to the police!"

"Yes, mom," he nodded.

"I mean it," Emma gave him a stern look. She didn't believe him.

"I said okay. I'll leave it to the police," he agreed.

Emma fluffed his pillows and straightened out his blankets. Then she began inspecting his IV site and the tubing.

"You know, I already have a nurse. You can sit down and just keep me company."

Emma shrugged then pulled a chair next to his bed and sat down.

"So — I met Joe yesterday."

"Uh, yeah, I heard." David pushed himself up in the bed and shifted uncomfortably. He was unsure how Emma felt about him being married to a man. After all, she did seem to have a slight crush on him.

"He's cute and seems very nice. I like him."

"He's a great guy. We served together in Afghanistan."

"Yeah, he mentioned that."

There was a period of silence. David felt unsure of what to say, he rarely talked to anyone about his relationship with Joe other than family and very close friends. He felt awkward speaking to Emma because he didn't know how she felt about the issue. But now that she knew, he thought he might as well be upfront with her.

"Listen, about Joe," David broke the silence. "I'm sorry I didn't say anything to you."

"That's okay, I understand why you didn't," she said.

"I just didn't know what to say. I had to spend my whole life hiding, from my family, from my friends, then from the military. I served under the 'Don't ask, don't tell' policy. Believe me, it wasn't as benign as it sounded. We had to keep quiet and stay hidden. The COs couldn't ask if a soldier was gay, but if they suspected it, they'd kick you out. And if the guys in my squad knew, God knows what they would have done."

"Was it really that bad? I thought the military didn't kick gays out anymore."

"Like I said, if we stayed in the closet and no one suspected, we were safe; but they sure as hell didn't tolerate it if they found out. So, I'm used to keeping my private life private."

"Sounds like someone else I know. Dr. Russo said the same thing."

"Really? Is he gay?" David sat up in his bed.

Emma laughed. "No. He's definitely not gay. He just said the same thing about keeping his private life private."

"It's a good policy. I'm afraid if people knew about me, they wouldn't be so accepting."

"This isn't the military. Most people don't care who you sleep with."

"Oh really." His expression hardened and clinched his teeth. "You've never been put in the hospital by a gang of rednecks just because they thought you looked gay."

"Did that happen to you?"

"Not to me, but it's happened to some of my friends. And, I've lost count of the number of calls I've been on where a poor guy was beaten to a pulp for looking gay. Seriously, you might think society is more tolerant, but it's not. Gay people are still getting fired from their jobs, and even getting killed."

"I'm sorry. Maybe you're right. Maybe there are people who would treat you differently if they knew. But there's others that wouldn't. You don't know how accepting people can be until you don't give them the chance."

"You don't know how cruel people can be either."

"Well, for what it's worth I'm very happy you have Joe. You make a very handsome couple."

"You mean that? I expected you'd be upset. You did sort of have the hots for me." David grinned at her. He was only half teasing. When she kissed him in the parking lot, it was evident that Emma was interested in him. Afterward he had attempted to avoid her so she wouldn't be encouraged; but they were just drawn to each other.

"I wouldn't go that far."

"Just admit it," David laughed. "You wanted me bad."

"Maybe just a little." Emma looked away and blushed. She was eager to change the subject from his teasing. "By the way, we haven't told anyone you're gay. It's your decision if, and when, you want anybody else to know."

"I appreciate that, but I'm afraid the cat's out of the bag. Joe was up here last night wailing and crying like I was on my deathbed."

"Oh, really? Poor guy. When he was in the waiting room, he was so worried about you."

"Well, maybe he wasn't all that bad," he admitted. "But he had to tell the nurses he was my husband so they would let him in. And he stayed the whole night. I'm sure it's all over the hospital by now."

Emma's phone chirped. She pulled it from her pocket and looked at the message.

"Something exciting?" David asked.

"I'm not sure. What's a victim of uh — " she hesitated and cleared her throat. "Uh, what's an ass gremlin?"

He laughed so hard he had to splint his side. "The victim of an ass gremlin?"

"Yes, what is one of those — those gremlin things?"

David pressed a pillow over his side and fought the urge to laugh. "The victim of an ass gremlin is someone who admits with a foreign body stuck inside their, uh, their rectum; but says they don't know how it got there."

"Oh boy, I guess I better get moving then," Emma laughed. "I'll check on you later today."

"See ya."

Emma patted him on the hand and headed out to the elevator. She had a bright smile and a bounce in her step. She felt closer to David now that he had shared his secret but was also a little disappointed that he turned out to be gay. He was ruggedly handsome, and a fantastic kisser. But she was all right with it, in fact, she was happy because now she believed they would be friends forever.

Had she dated David for a few weeks it could have ended badly. This way, with David being gay, she would have him as a friend much longer than she would have him as a boyfriend.

Emma stepped into the elevator and pushed the button for the first floor. Just as the doors started to close, she saw Sister Faith running toward the elevator.

"Hold please!" Sister Faith raised her hand and shouted like she was calling a taxi.

Emma pushed the hold button until Sister Faith jumped in.

"Thank you, dear," Sister Faith said. "These elevators are so slow today I was afraid I'd have to take the stairs, and my old bones can deal with that today."

Emma just smiled back at her.

"I understand we had some trouble in the emergency room yesterday," the sister said. "Terrible. Just terrible."

"Yes, it was very frightening for the whole staff."

"That poor paramedic. What is his name again?"

"David Marshall."

"Yes, that's it. He's such a sweet young man. All the sisters said a special prayer for his recovery this morning."

"I'm sure he'll appreciate knowing that."

The elevator bell dinged, and the doors opened onto the 1st floor.

"Well, good day dear," Sister Faith said as they exited the elevator."

"Excuse me Sister, a quick question if you have a moment."

"Yes, dear?"

"Would there be any problem if you found out an employee was gay? I mean would he have to worry about his job or anything?".

Sister Faith eyes narrowed with curiosity. "Oh dear, has someone been harassing you?"

"No, no, no." Emma couldn't help but laugh that Sister Faith thought she was asking for herself. "No, it's not me. I was just wondering. I have a friend who is thinking of apply for a job here."

"He shouldn't be concerned about that. Frankly, dear, if we didn't hire homosexuals, we'd lose half our staff." She gave a belly laugh. "Now, go tell your friend to fill out an application and you can bring it directly to me."

"Thank you, sister." Having decided it was none of her business, it was comforting to know that if gossip was spreading, David wouldn't have to worry about losing his job.

Back at the Emergency Department Emma checked in with Pam at the nursing station.

"Where do you need me?" She asked Pam.

"Room 4. Dr. Myers has ordered a K-Y enema," Pam smirked.

"Are you serious? A full enema with K-Y?"

"Romeo said he was unpacking groceries in the nude when he slipped and fell onto a Gatorade bottle."

"He has a Gatorade bottle up his — up his bottom?" Emma gasped.

"You betcha. Doc Myers said to give him a liter of K-Y by enema and see if he can push it out on his own, otherwise it's off to surgery."

"Does K-Y even come in a liter bottle? I've only seen the small packets on the cart."

"We have the two-ounce tubes on the med carts. You'll need to open a couple dozen tubes and squeeze them in a bag."

Dr. Myers was sitting at the nursing station documenting in a patient's chart. She was a young Asian female who normally worked the weekends but was there covering for Finn so he could have the day off. She reminded Emma of Margaret Cho with her very animated facial expressions and a naughty sense of humor.

"Doctor Myers," Emma addressed her.

"Yes, my little one." Myers replied playfully. That's what she affectionately called Emma since she was so young and petite.

"The patient in room 4, with the foreign object. Do you mind if I use ultrasound gel instead of K-Y as a lubricant for the enema? It should work just as well as and it already comes in a bottle."

"That's a good idea. Write the verbal order, and I'll cosigned it later. Frankly, I'd could just give him a bottle of poppers and let him get it out himself the same way he got it in. But then we couldn't charge his insurance company a fortune."

The nurses laughed as Doctor Myers walked away.

Emma leaned toward Pam and asked in a subdued voice, "what's a bottle of poppers?"

"Oh please," Kenise cackled loudly. "If you don't know, then you don't need to know."

"I think you guys love giving me all the bizarre patients just to see my reaction," Emma said as she collected the patient's chart.

"You think?" Kenise leaned back and glared at Emma. "Why don't you take a little stroll down to my patient in trauma six. You will recognize him by the fishhook in his eye. Then let me know if you'd like to trade patients."

"I've got a 90-year-old with a vaginal yeast infection and candida growing like moss under both breasts." Pam added. "You can take her if you like and I'll do the butt guy."

"Okay, point taken. I'll do the enema."

CHAPTER 14

"Girl, look at you," Kenise said as Emma arrived at the time clock wearing blue scrubs instead of her usual white nursing uniform. "You decide you wanted to be a real nurse today?"

"I've stained every one of my white uniforms as of yesterday. I decided that scrubs are half the price, easier to clean, and last twice as long." Emma smiled.

"TGIF." Pam joined the group that was waiting to clock in.

"Praise his name," Kenise shouted and raised her hands to heaven. "I've got big plans for this weekend. I plan to soak in a tub full of Epsom salts, drink some Chardonnay, and read this month's Harlequin novel. And nobody better not call me to come in to this place."

"I hear ya," Pam laughed. "I'm turning my phone off. What about you, Emma? Anything exciting on your schedule."

Dr. Russo stepped around the corner. "Yeah, she's buying me a steak dinner."

All the nurses' eyes widen in surprise. It was highly unusual for Dr. Russo to include himself in their conversations, much less to openly flirt in front of the staff.

"Oh, really?" Kenise placed her hand on her hip and gave Emma a motherly glare. "What's been going on behind my back?"

"Nothing," Emma blushed. For all the times he said he liked to keep his private life private, it surprised her that Finn would be so bold in front of the nurses.

"You owe me a dinner, remember?" He persisted. "And I'm not eating until you pay up, so be ready for a hungry man's appetite."

"Then you'll lose a lot of weight from starvation," Emma smirked at him. "Cause I'm not buying you dinner."

"Then my death is on your hands," he pretended to stab himself in the heart then walked away.

Both Pam and Kenise crossed her arms and glared at her.

"What?" Emma asked.

"You've been holding out on us," Pam said. "Seems no one told you, but if you work in the ER, we don't hide things from each other. Especially if it involved a tall glass of water like that man."

"Spill the beans, girlfriend," Kenise said. "What is going on, how long has it been going on, and how far has he gotten?"

"I'm serious. Nothing is going on. We simply had a bet, and I lost."

"A bet?" Kenise asked.

Emma didn't want to tell them the nature of the bet since it would involve revealing that David was gay. "It was just something silly. I'm not going out with him."

"Honey, to be blunt, you'd be a fool not to." Pam remarked.

"Hell. I'd buy him a steak dinner every night if he'd look at me the way he looks at you." Kenise said and laughed. "Listen, baby. You go out with that man. I don't care if you have to sell your plasma to pay for it, you buy that man dinner."

"That's right," Pam agreed. "And I'd throw in a movie and a hotel room to boot."

"Excuse me ladies," another nurse interrupted. "Time to clock in."

"We're not finished with this," Kenise assured Emma as she punched her time card.

As the group walked toward the main nursing station, a man wearing a hoody and carrying a backpack bumped into Pam as he hurried past the group. He didn't say a word, but just kept going.

"How rude," Pam said to the other women. "Didn't even say excuse me."

"These young kids today have no manners," Kenise shook her head in disgust. "If that were my child, I'd box his jaws right then and there."

"Did he look familiar to you?" Emma asked. There was something familiar in his appearance though she didn't get a good look at his face.

"He had that hood over his head and his pants down to his knees," Kenise scoffed. "Looks like every other hoodlum in this city."

"Well, it's a generational thing," Pam said. "I don't get it, but a lot of the kids seem to dress that way."

"And a lot of kids need to have a switch taken to their legs too." Kenise continued.

Emma excused herself from the conversation and looked at the patient assignment board. There were only three patients currently in rooms. Emma looked at the board and saw she was assigned which patient she was assigned to then proceeded to the room to relieve the night shift nurse.

"Good morning," Emma said as she entered the patient room.

The night nurse was just hanging a new IV bag on the pole at the head of the patient's bed.

"Hello," Jackie, the night nurse greeted her. "I haven't me to yet. You must be Emma."

"Yes, I'm Emma Paige. I'm your relief this morning."

"Oh good. I'm ready to go home."

"Busy night?" Emma asked

"No, not at all. It's been slow as a morgue, so the night just dragged by. We've spent most the night restocking carts, arranging files, and holding each other's eyelids open."

Emma laughed. "Sorry. The shift does seem to go much faster when you're busy."

Emma glanced at the patient lying asleep on the bed. It was a middle-aged white male who appeared to be in good physical condition, like a powerlifter or bodybuilder. Otherwise, there was nothing remarkable about his physical appearance. When she looked at the monitor, she could readily see why he was a patient. His heart rate was steady at 85 beats per minute, but the EKG complex was clearly abnormal. The last segment of the QRS wave, called the ST segment, was significantly elevated taking the shape of little tombstones.

"Oh, I can see the issue here." Emma remarked.

Jackie motioned for her to step outside into the hallway and Emma followed. The she began to give Emma the patient report.

"He came in this morning around 4 a.m. Drove himself believe it or not." Jackie said. "He was complaining a severe heart burn and when the triage nurse checked his pulse and blood pressure she about fainted. He had a pressure of 230 over 140."

"Oh wow. He looks so healthy."

"He admitted to using steroids along with a grocery list of supplements for working out. And there you have the results, a perfect body with a busted heart. He'll go up to the Cardiac Unit as soon as they finish with shift report. He's had morphine and has been sleeping like a baby for the past hour. All you need to do is watch the monitor until the transport team shows up to take him off your hands."

As they were finishing up report, the young man in the hoodie walked by headed back to the front lobby. This time Emma saw his face clearly, and she recognized him.

"Sir," Emma called out to him.

He didn't respond but stated to walk faster toward the ambulance entrance.

"Sir!" She called out again and started after him.

This time he glanced back. When he saw her, he started running and was quickly out the door.

Emma rushed to the desk where the staff was still engaged in their shift report. "Did you see him?" She was panting and her heart racing.

"See who?" Pam asked.

"That kid. The one with the hoodie." "That was the kid that stabbed David."

"Oh, my god!" Pam exclaimed. "Where did he go?"

"When he saw I recognized him he took off running out the ambulance entrance into the parking lot." Emma stated.

"Belinda, call security stat to the ER," Pam told the desk clerk.

"What the heck was he doing here anyway?" Kenise asked.

"Remember? He threatened Dr. Russo," Pam said. "He said something about if his friend died that he would die."

"Oh my God! Has anybody seen Dr. Russo?" Kenise shouted and raced from behind the desk and frantically calling out, "Dr. Russo! Dr. Russo!"

"What's the problem?" Finn stepped out of one of the patient rooms.

"Thank God!" Emma clutched her neck in relief.

Finn walked down the hall to the nursing station. "What's going on? What's all the shouting about?"

"That kid that threatened you a couple days ago. The one that stabbed David." Pam was so flustered and upset she had to stop and catch her breath.

"What about him?" Russo asked.

"He was just here walking around," Emma said. "We thought he might be looking for you."

"You mean that kid that was wondering around earlier with the hoodie and the backpack?" Finn asked. "He must not have been looking for me, he walked right past me in the hallway and didn't even look up."

"Pam," Emma's face turned ghostly white.

"Emma? What's wrong?" Pam noticed the color drain from Emma's face.

"When he ran out, he wasn't carrying a backpack." Emma's voice trembled.

"Are you sure?" Pam's ears turned bright red and her hands began to quiver.

"Yes! I'm sure. He wasn't carrying a backpack." Emma insisted.

"Are you certain he came in with one?" Kenise asked. "Think are you sure he had a backpack?"

"Yes. I saw it."

"He definitely was carrying a backpack when he passed by me." Finn agreed.

Pam grabbed the phone from the desk and pressed zero. "We have a Code Black situation in the ER. This is not a drill. Call 911 and get the fire and police departments here."

By the time Pam had put the phone back on the receiver everyone's cell phone sounded a loud alert tone, and immediately afterward the overhead PA system was blaring, "Code Black. Code Black. Code Black. This is not a drill."

As the charge nurse, Pam had been trained for this type of situation, so she immediately started barking orders. "I want everyone evacuated into the parking lot. Kenise can you shut off the oxygen valve. Can someone get some oxygen tanks from the storage closet?"

"I'll get the tanks," Dr. Russo volunteered.

"Great, let's get moving everybody!" Pam urged.

The entire staff responded quickly. Kenise ran to the back hallway and closed the oxygen valve and quickly returned to help Emma prepare to evacuate her cardiac patient. As they pushed the patient into the hall, Emma saw Finn bolt out of the storage closet where the oxygen cylinders were kept. From his expression she could see that something was wrong.

"Everybody out now!" Finn shouted at the top of his lungs. He ran down the hallway toward Emma but made it only a few yards when there was an explosion from within the storage closet. The blast blew the door clean out of its frame almost hitting Finn as he rushed to get away.

Then there was a second explosion, and a fireball blasted through the wall sending flames and debris shooting outward. The entire building seemed to shake and the impact threw Finn to the floor. Emma and Kenise dove against a wall covered their heads to shield themselves from the flying debris.

Everyone was in a state of shock and confusion; their ears were ringing from the blast and the patient on the stretcher was clutching his chest and crying out in fear.

Both women rose to their feet cautiously. Emma looked up the hallway and saw Finn climbing to his feet. He seemed disoriented and confused.

Emma's ears were ringing from the sound of the explosion when the fire alarm began to blare loudly. Then the sprinkler system activated. The department was in chaos. Over the sound of the alarms and screams, there was a distinct, loud popping sound.

"What is that?" Emma turned to Kenise. "Is that — "

"God help us!" Kenise responded. "That's gunshots."

The sound of the gunfire was coming from near the ambulance entrance which meant they couldn't evacuate to the parking lot as planned. To get to either the visitor's entrance or the entrance to the main hospital, they would have to pass by the ambulance entrance which again left them completely exposed if there was a gunman in the area. The only other exit available to them was the back stairwell, but to reach it they had to go past the storage room which was already engulfed in flames. They had no choice; all they could do was find a secure place to hide until help arrived.

"Quick, get the patient back in the room!" Emma shouted.

"No, we gotta get out of here!" The patient said and then jumped off the stretcher. He was about to run toward the exit when Kenise grabbed him.

"Listen," Kenise said firmly. "You go down that way and you're going to get shot. We need to get back in the room and keep your mouth shut!"

He hesitated, but there was the sound of someone screaming followed by two rapid gunshots. That was enough to send Kenise and the patient running back into the room. Meanwhile, Emma ran to help Finn who was stumbling down the hallway toward her. She put her arm around him and together followed Kenise into the treatment room and closed the door behind them.

"Are you all right?" She asked as she helped Finn to sit on the floor and rest against the wall.

"Yeah, I think so," he nodded. "I pulled my back when I fell."

"Try not to move." Emma searched for something to use to block the door, but everything large enough to block the door was either bolted to the floor or on wheels. She found two rubber door stops and wedged them tightly under the door. Once they were in place, she pulled at the door to make sure the stops would hold. Then used surgical tape to tape a towel over the glass so the shooter couldn't see into the room.

"Emma," Kenise called to her in a hushed voice even though the sound of the fire alarm made it impossible for anyone outside the room to hear her. "Emma."

"Sssh," Emma whispered as she lightly pulled the towel back and peered cautiously through the glass window of the door. She could see the flames from the storage room fire. The water from the sprinklers was helping to slow the spread but the fractured gas cylinders were spewing enough oxygen to keep the fire active. She knew that if the fire continued, they couldn't stay in the room much longer, but neither could they risk trying to leave.

Suddenly, Kenise's phone rang. She quickly silenced it, and everyone held their breath in fear that the ringing may have betrayed their location. Emma peeked out the door window then sighed when saw no one approaching.

Kenise checked her phone and turned it to vibrate. "It was Pam calling, I'll text her and see if she's okay."

Kenise typed a quick message then waited for a response. A moment later the phone vibrated briefly and Kenise read the reply. "Thank God! She made it outside."

Another text came through. "She says the police are outside and there's a swat team on the way. She asked if we know how many gunmen?"

"I don't know. I've not seen anyone, just heard shots." Emma pulled back the towel again and peeked into the hallway. The fire was still burning but still there was no sign of the shooter. Suddenly, there was the sound of rapid gunfire that made Emma jump to the floor while Kenise muffled her own scream by putting her hand over her mouth. The gunfire seemed to be closer than it was before.

Kenise emerged from her corner to join Emma at the door. "The shots sound closer now," she whispered so that the patient wouldn't hear. "He's going room to room."

"Oh god," Emma gasped.

Together they peered out at the door down the hallway. It was getting harder to see through the smoke. Emma squinted her eyes and struggled to see the door to the stairwell just past the smoldering storage area. "I think we can make it to the stairs, go down to the basement and exit from there."

"Don't you think we need to stay put?" Kenise asked.

"The smoke's getting thicker and if the shooter is heading toward us, I don't think we can wait."

Kenise grabbed a box of N95 masks from the supply cart. "We can use these. They should filter enough of the smoke for us to make it to the door. If we cover ourselves with wet sheets, I think we can make it."

"It might work," Kenise said. "It's better than staying here like sitting ducks."

"What about him? You think he can make it?" Emma asked and motioned toward the cardiac patient still in the corner.

"Yeah, I can make it," the man answered. "I'm not staying here."

"Finn, you want to do this?" Emma turned to see him slumped back against the wall where she had left him. "Finn, you okay?"

"Yeah." He grimaced with pain and seemed confused. "I can make it."

"Let's do it while we have the chance," Kenise said.

They grabbed the sheets and wet them in the sink. Emma dislodged the rubber stops she had wedged under the door. Kenise helped the patient to his feet and then slipped one of the N95 masks over his nose and mouth. She took a wet sheet and wrapped it around him then put on her own mask.

"You ready?" Emma asked.

Kenise nodded her head. Emma slowly opened the door just enough to look down the hallway. She saw no one.

"It's clear," Emma whispered. "You go first then Finn and I will follow."

Again, she opened the door slowly and peeked out to make sure the coast was clear. "Go!" Emma urged.

Kenise and Jon darted out the door and headed into the thick smoke. Emma watched through the window as they hurried past the fire, down the hall and into the stairwell. She breathed a sigh of relief as they disappeared into the stairwell and the door closed behind them.

"They made it," Emma informed Finn. "Are you ready?"

She grabbed him by the arm to help him to his feet. He tried to stand but fell back to the floor. Then she noticed blood smeared on the wall directly behind where Finn was resting his back.

"Finn? You're bleeding."

"I don't think I have a pulled back muscle after all," he said in a weak voice.

Emma squatted on the floor beside him and gently leaned him forward to get a look at his back. She gasped when she saw the lower portion of his lab coat soaked with blood. "Oh God! You're bleeding!"

"Yeah, we've established that fact."

He coughed and when he did, blood sprayed from his mouth.

"Let's get your lab coat and shirt off so I can see what is going on?" Emma didn't wait for his consent. She took a pair of scissors from her scrub pocket and quickly cut through the clothing to expose his upper body. She assisted him in leaning forward so she could have a better view of his back.

There was a gaping wound on the right side of his back just below the scapula. The wound was oozing blood and each time he took a breath the wound bubbled.

Emma was so frightened and concerned she felt herself close to passing out. She braced her arm against the wall and took several deep breaths to regain her composure. Once she had collected herself, she refocused her attention to Finn.

"Honey, I need you to lie down on your stomach so I can get a closer look. Can you do that for me?"

Suddenly there was the sound of gunfire again. Five rapid shots one after the other. Emma covered her mouth to avoid screaming in terror. They remained silent waiting to see if the gunman was approaching.

"Emma," Finn grabbed her by the wrist and looked in her eyes. "You need to go while you still can."

"No, I'm not leaving you. You can lean on me. We'll go together."

"I'm sorry, I don't think I can make it." He struggled for air as he spoke. "Please Emma. I beg of you. I need to know that you're safe."

"No! You can't ask me to leave you hear." She was almost in tears. "I won't do it."

"Emma. You need to get out while you can. Please, I beg of you. Once you're outside, you can send help."

She didn't want to leave him; but his condition was rapidly deteriorating, and he needed help. She began to sob, fearing that if she didn't get help, he would die but just as frightened to leave him to die alone.

"Please, Emma. For me."

She leaned over and kissed him. She stood and began to back away. She pulled the N95 mask over her face then took one of the wet sheets from the sink and wrapped it around her.

"I'll bring help," she promised as she paused at the door.

"Just get out of here!"

She gave him a nod and one final tearful glance, then slowly opened the door and looked out. Seeing the path was still clear, she dashed out the door.

CHAPTER 15

Finn felt his chest tightening, and it was becoming harder to breathe. As an emergency physician, he knew what was happening, and he knew that he was dying. What he had thought was a pulled back muscle when he fell was something much worse, it was shrapnel from the explosion. The blast had sent debris flying in all directions and one projectile had pierced his back like a bullet. From his labored breathing, Finn realized that whatever had hit him had penetrated his lung and caused his lung to collapse.

He saw an oxygen tank underneath the patient stretcher and attempted to slide toward it. If he could reach the tank, he could use the oxygen help him breathe, and hopefully buy some time for help to arrive. He was too weak from the lack of oxygen and loss of blood to make it to the stretcher and he collapsed face down on the floor. His vision blurred, and the room seemed to grow darker until he lost consciousness.

Finn woke to find an oxygen mask on his face, and he was lying flat on his stomach with his head turned to the side. He could see a shadowy figure next to him. As his eyes refocused, he saw that it was Emma.

"You didn't leave," he mumbled. "Why?"

"Why do you think?" She answered sharply.

Emma had made it all the way to the stairwell, but she couldn't bring herself to go through the door. She flashed back to the moment when Brock was dying in her arms on the mountain. She couldn't help him because she didn't know what to do other than to comfort him. That moment had changed the course of her life. She promised herself that she would never feel that powerless again, and that's why she fought so hard to get into nursing school. That's why she neglected her social life in favor of studying.

She couldn't allow herself to leave Finn behind; she realized that if she left Finn alone and dying, all she had worked for would have been for nothing. She could not bring herself to leave him any more than she could have left Brock alone on that mountaintop.

Emma kneeled beside him on the floor and gently positioned him on his side so she could examine the wound. "I need to look at your back," she said as she slipped on a pair of sterile gloves. "I'll be as gentle as I can, but it might hurt a little."

She inspected the gaping hole in his back. Something had ripped into the flesh and she could see the object protruding from inside the wound. Gently, she used her fingers to open the gash and get a better look at it. It was a chunk of metal from an oxygen cylinder.

"Finn honey. There's a piece of metal still in your back. I need to try and get it out."

Finn did not respond. He had fallen unconscious and was gasping for air. With each breath he took, blood bubbled within the wound as the air was being pulled into it. She recognized the clinical symptoms. He had a sucking-chest wound, a life-threatening emergency where air is pulled in through the wound rather than the upper airways. This caused his lung to collapse and the expanding pressure in his chest cavity was preventing him from getting air into his lungs. Emma knew if she didn't do something quickly, he would die in a matter of minutes.

"Finn, can you hear me?" She shook his shoulders but there was no response.

Emma felt herself panicking. She was on her own with no one to tell her what to do, and Finn was dying right before her eyes. She had to do something. She ran to the crash cart and took a pair of hemostats from the top drawer then hurried back to Finn. Using the hemostats, she gently reached inside the wound and pulled the metal shard out. She looked at it closely; it was a thick green piece of metal.

"Part of an oxygen cylinder," she said aloud and dropped it to the floor.

With the removal of the metal, the wound poured with blood and the gas bubbles became more pronounced. She remembered from her training that the emergency treatment for a sucking-chest wound was to block it using a vented chest seal. Fortunately, she recalled exactly where those were located on the trauma cart. She opened the cart and dug through the equipment until she found one. Using a stack of gauze and Betadine from the cart she cleaned around the wound then dried the surrounding skin as much as she could with it still bleeding.

She opened the package of the chest seal and quickly scanned the instructions on the outside of the packaging. It was a simple device; a small plastic one-way valve with an adhesive backing that would cover the wound. Once in place it would prevent air from entering the chest though the puncture while allowing trapped air to escape, thus relieving the pressure within the chest cavity and allowing the lung to re-expand.

Her hands were trembling as she tried to peel the paper from the adhesive ring. In her nervous rush, she dropped the valve to the floor.

"Contaminated," she growled as she picked it back up. "That's what antibiotics are for."

"Please, please, please," she mumbled as she carefully used her fingernail to remove the paper from the adhesive. She used another clean gauze to wipe around the wound then pressed the valve over the puncture.

Immediately, she saw the valve close as Finn inhaled then reopen when he exhaled along with the fait sound of air escaping. With each breath, Finn's breathing became less labored and took on a more rhythmic and natural pattern. The valve was working; the wound was closed, and Finn's lung was re-expanding.

"Thank you, God," she said with relief and sank to the floor beside him. She pulled him close and rested his head in her lap. He was still unconscious, but she didn't attempt to rouse him. Instead, she let him rest. It would serve no purpose for him to be awake at that moment. Whether it was the smoke that finally took them, or the gunman; she decided it would be more merciful if he was not awake when it happened.

She sat in the floor holding him. She thought back to when she did the same for Brock when he had died. This time was different, she was not helpless. She had saved Finn's life.

There was the sound of gunfire again. This time she didn't jump. The sound of the fire alarm continued to blare loudly, and she had grown numb to both the alarm and the gunshots.

Suddenly the door burst open. Emma closed her eyes tightly and pulled Finn close to her. She was prepared to die.

"We have two more survivors," a male voice shouted.

When she opened her eyes and saw the officer in combat gear standing in the doorway, she began to cry. They had survived

CHAPTER 16

Emma planted her skis in the snow and looked about her. Something seemed odd. There was a strong sense of déjà vu. She had been here before, at that very moment. It wasn't just a feeling of having lived that moment before, she knew she had. She recognized the place and she felt her stomach quiver with dread. Something awful was about to happen, but what it was eluded her.

She looked up the ski slope knowing at any moment Brock would come bounding over the hill. She prayed he would not come; but a second later there he was. Springing over the hill and taking to the air momentarily as he did.

When he raced past her, Brock leaned onto the edge of his skis spraying snow powder in her face as he went. He glanced back and laughed loudly when he saw her dusting the snow off her face.

"Race you down!" He called back to her then leaned forward into the skis to pick up speed.

With a push from the poles she darted after him. She was an experienced skier but not as fast as Brock, and much more cautious. By the time she could get moving he was already over the next knoll and out of her vision. He was going too fast, she thought. There was a clump of trees just ahead there was a and the ski slope took a turn, Brock was going too fast to get safely around the bend.

When she got to the top of the next hill, she saw the trees, but she didn't see Brock. She knew he couldn't have gotten that far ahead of her. Stopping halfway down the hill, she paused and looked around but didn't see him anywhere. She spotted the fresh ski tracks in the new fallen snow and began to slowly follow them toward the patch of trees. All the while a sense of dread grew in her gut.

She glided through the trees following the ski tracks until they ended right at a fallen tree. She unclipped her skis from her boots so she could climb over it. Then she saw Brock lying in the snow just behind the heavy trunk. He was on his side and motionless; one of his legs was twisted into an awkward position and a sharp bone was piercing through his pant leg just above the knee. Blood stained the snow extending nearly a foot beyond where he lay. When the bone broke and pierced the skin, it had torn open an artery causing blood to spurt from the wound.

"Brock!" She cried out and fell to the ground next to him.

She pulled his head and shoulders onto her lap. He was gasping for breath. He looked blankly back at her and tried to speak, but no words came from his mouth. There was a deep laceration on the side of his head and blood streaming from his ear.

She didn't scream, nor cry out again. She tenderly stroked his hair to comfort him. She knew he was dying; she remembered it and she knew there was nothing she could do to help him. So rather than fight what was happening, she comforted him and accepted it.

"I'm here," she said lovingly. "Everything will be all right."

Brock's breathing slowed, and he was no longer struggling. He closed his eyes as if he were going to sleep and then was gone. Emma looked up into the sky and cried, feeling the heartbreaking loss all over again. When she looked back down at him, it was no longer

Brock she saw resting in her lap. It was Finn.

"No, no, no!" Emma cried out.

A moment later the falling snow faded away and the surrounding air became warm. The grey clouds that had darkened the sky evaporated revealing a vibrant blue sky overhead. The snow that had covered the earth melted away, leaving a lush green landscape bathed in dandelions and wild flowers. She was no longer in the cold winter but found herself in the midst of a perfect spring day.

She looked toward the sun as it rose over the ridge a short distance away. The light was so bright she brought her hand to her face to shield her eyes. Then she saw someone standing in the distance at the top of the ridge bathed in the bright sunshine.

It was Brock. He looked back at her with a beaming smile and waved, then he turned and walked away until he vanished into the sunlight.

Emma awoke in a recliner sitting next to Finn's bed in the I.C.U. The dream had been so vivid that she awoke confused and struggled for a moment to remember where she was.

"Bad dream?" Finn asked when he saw her awake. He was laying in the hospital bed, an IV in one arm, a nasal oxygen cannula under his nose, and electrodes on his chest. "I didn't know if I should wake you or let you rest."

"Yeah, it was," she replied but quickly changed her mind. "Actually, no, it wasn't really a bad dream. Well, I'm not sure."

"Wanna talk about it?"

"No, it was just so vivid." She rubbed her eyes, and the confusion dissipated. "So how are feeling?"

"For having a hole in my back I'm feeling fairly well. I guess I have you to thank for that."

"No thanks necessary." She stretched and gave a yawn.

"Hey, I owe you my life. When I said you needed to prove yourself as a nurse, I didn't expect you to risk your life to yank me from the jaws of death."

"Does this mean you trust me now?"

"With my life, babe." He took her hand and held it tightly. "You've been here all night with me. You need to go home and rest."

"I think I'll stick around for a while longer if you don't mind."

"Why?"

"I think you know why." She gently brushed his hair from off his face. "You need a trim, you're too handsome to hide behind all that hair."

"You can cut it for me when I get out of here."

She continued to stroke his hair and run her fingers through it while they held hands.

"Emma," Finn said in a soft voice. "I want to apologize to you.

"For what? For being a jerk when I first started working here? For making everyone call me Nurse Enema? Making fun of my nursing uniforms? Or trying to freeze me out after I turned you down for dinner?"

She was only teasing him. She had already forgiven him, and she would never look back at that again.

"For all of it. I'm sorry for the way I behaved. I am the most imperfect man you'll ever meet, and I make a lot of mistakes. I wish I could say that I will never hurt you, or make you mad, be insensitive, or make you cry. But I know I will."

"Well that's comforting," she laughed.

"Just know that when I do screw up it's out of ignorance and not intentional. The last thing I want to do is to cause you sorrow. I may not notice a new dress or your shoes, or when you first change your hairstyle … but know that to me you will always be beautiful no matter how you look or what you wear. I will always notice the way you light up a room when you enter. I will always notice the love in your eyes and the beauty in your face. I know I'm going to screw up, probably a lot. But I also know that you are my heart. When you hurt, I will hurt. When you cry, I will cry with you."

"Oh, my." She placed her hand over her heart and her eyes filled with tears. She sat back in the chair and took a deep breath to gather her thoughts, and her feelings.

"You don't need to say anything now." He saw that she was hesitant to speak. "I didn't mean to make you uncomfortable, it's just that I haven't been able to get you out of my head since that night when I walked you home. And after what we went through, I don't want another day to pass without you knowing how I feel. I love you, Nurse Paige."

The was silence. Finn waited expectantly for her to say something. She stared straight ahead thoughtfully for a long while.

"I've changed my mind." She finally spoke.

"About?"

"I think I would like to have dinner with you after all."